Ozark
Tales & and
Superstitions

Also by Phillip W. Steele

The Last Cherokee Warriors, 1974

Jesse and Frank James: The Family History, 1987

Starr Tracks: Belle and Pearl Starr, 1989

The Many Faces of Jesse James, 1995

Outlaws and Gunfighters of the Old West, 1991

Civil War in the Ozarks, 1993
(coauthored with Steve Cottrell)

Ozark Tales

and
Superstitions

PHILLIP W. STEELE

Illustrations by
Donna Chapman and Erwin Doege

PELICAN PUBLISHING COMPANY
GRETNA 1998

Library of Congress Cataloging in Publication Data
Steele. Phillip W.
    Ozark tales and superstitions.

    1. Tales—Ozark Mountains Region. 2. Folklore—
Ozark Mountains Region. 3. Ozark Mountains Region—
Social life and customs. I. Title.
GR110.M77S73 1983   398.2'09767'1   82-22425
ISBN 0-88289-404-8

First printing, May 1983
Second printing, May 1985
Third printing, March 1988
Fourth printing, March 1998

Manufactured in the United States of America

Published by Pelican Publishing Company, Inc.
200 Newton Street, Gretna, Louisiana 70053

Dedicated to the memory of my grandparents,
Joseph Dalton Gilliland (1880–1972)
and
Irena Ann Gilliland (1884–1967),
second-generation Ozark natives. The tales
they told and the beliefs they held encouraged
me to try to preserve our Ozark folk heritage.

Contents

Preface

The Ozark Mountain range embraces northern Arkansas and southern Missouri, reaches into the southern tip of Illinois, and gently spreads into northeastern Oklahoma and southeastern Kansas. Geologists tell us that the Ozarks are among the oldest mountain ranges in the nation.

Many stories are told about how the name "Ozark" originated, and although the theories differ slightly it is now generally agreed that the term is derived from the name given to the area by early French and Spanish explorers. Whether it was DeSoto himself or a later French explorer, someone began to refer to the area as the land of the bows—"aux arcs" in French—because of the exceptionally strong and beautiful bows fashioned by the Indians of the region. Another theory suggests that the term refers to the "bois d'arc" or bowwood tree, which the Indians used to make these bows.

The Osage, Choctaw, and other Indian tribes were the original inhabitants of the Ozarks. A part of the Louisiana Purchase of 1803, the area was opened for white settlement soon thereafter. In an attempt to encourage the Cherokee Nation of Georgia, Tennessee, and the Carolinas to move further west voluntarily, lands in North Arkansas were granted to them by treaty in 1810. But only 4,000 members of the tribe moved, and it was not until the late 1830s that the Indian Removal Acts forced the migration of the Cherokees to the lands that are now eastern Oklahoma.

Shortly after these Indian removals more settlers began coming to the Ozarks. Most were of Dutch, Irish, Welsh, or Scottish descent and were following the trails west from the Virginias, Carolinas, and Tennessee. Considerable inter-marriage took place between the new white settlers and those Osage and Cherokee Indians who had remained in the region. This blending of cultures created a unique social environment and a heritage that still influences Ozark society today.

9

The abundance of water, timber, and wildlife in the Ozarks and the natural beauty of the lush green hills and meadows offered the early immigrants a virtual paradise. But life was also hard and lonely, since farms were scattered many miles apart with few roads through the rugged terrain. For people living hundreds of miles from any settlement other than the occasional trading post, organized social activity was virtually nonexistent. Still, the basic human desire for entertainment had to be fulfilled; storytelling soon became common.

Some Ozark folktales were undoubtedly based on fact. Most, however, became greatly altered and exaggerated as they were told over and over and passed from generation to generation. In compiling this work I have not been concerned about whether any tale was based on fact or was a pure fabrication. Few of these tales have ever been written down; they were commonly told only from memory. It is, therefore, one of the purposes of this text to preserve in print examples of how our forebears entertained themselves by creating drama, mystery, excitement, and emotion through the literary transformation of their natural surroundings.

Just as the structure of early Ozark society encouraged the development of the folktale, the mysterious atmosphere of the haze-covered Ozark Mountains nurtured the early settlers' natural tendency toward superstitious thinking. In fact, more superstitions seem to have survived in the Ozarks than in any other part of North America. For the most part the superstitions recorded in this book either originated within early Ozark society or were more widely believed in this region than anywhere else in the country.

Television, radio, stereo, books, movies, travel, concerts, sporting events, and the hundreds of other ways we find to entertain ourselves today leave little time for the passing on of traditional tales of wonder, and the technological, educational, and scientific advances of the twentieth century have resulted in diminished interest in superstitious belief. These important aspects of our folk heritage may, therefore, soon be lost forever. Other parts of our culture such as folk music, folk arts and crafts, architecture, and folk dance are being preserved through practice and demonstration by many Ozark natives. Our oral traditions deserve the same respect. It is my hope that this work might make others more aware of the importance of recording folktales and superstitions within their families and communities. By finding time in our busy lives to spin a good yarn—or better yet, to write down a story or record a tradition for future generations—we can help preserve this precious part of our cultural past.

Acknowledgments

I would like to thank the following people for their assistance and support in preparing this collection: Bruce Seaton, Galena, Missouri (The Legend of Virgin's Bluff), Walter Mayes; Goshen, Arkansas, and Ralph Mayes, Fayetteville, Arkansas (The Treasure of Mill Ford Hollow); Q. B. Boydstun, Fort Gibson, Oklahoma (The Legend of Vivia); Doyle Reed, Springdale, Arkansas (Tales of Callahan Mountain); G. S. Lambert, Hickory Creek, Arkansas (Jewels of the Devil); L. O. Lester, Westville, Oklahoma (Belle Starr's Horse Race and The Ozarks' Last Horseback Outlaw); Carl Bunch, Springdale, Arkansas (The Ozarks' Last Horseback Outlaw and Kingston's First Telephone); Gloria Farley, Eastern Oklahoma Historical Society, Heavener, Oklahoma (Heavener Runestones); and Hugh Bunch, Kingston, Arkansas (Kingston's First Telephone).

FOLKTALES

There are several distinct categories of Ozark folktales and hundreds of stories within each category. Among the most common categories are supernatural tales, lost treasure tales, Civil War stories, Indian legends, outlaw stories, tales about nature, tales of romance, and humorous stories. Most tales within any category are similar to one another, with only a few details changed. Examples of tales from each category have been selected for presentation here.

Folktales are for the most part old stories that have been passed from one generation to the next for many years, although a few new tales are still being created.

Tales of the Supernatural

The Legend of Ghost Hollow

The beautiful month of October ends with Halloween, the one night each year we traditionally recognize ghosts, goblins, and witches within our midst. There is perhaps no better place than the Ozarks in which to celebrate this ancient holiday, for few areas in our nation can boast such an abundance of ghost stories. The legend of Ghost Hollow is one example of the hundreds of ghost stories still told throughout the region.

Judge David Walker of Fayetteville, Arkansas, was a leader in Arkansas state government and served as a justice of the Arkansas Supreme Court for many years. In 1872 Judge Walker selected a spot on Fayetteville's East Mountain on which to build a two-story brick home as a wedding present for his daughter Mary and her husband, Senator J. D. Walker. When they moved into their beautiful new home, the Walkers found it very difficult to keep domestic help. They employed several black descendants of early Fayetteville slaves, but soon found that most of these servants would not stay long and were most reluctant to stay overnight at the home. The servants' fear stemmed from a bizarre tale about the house site.

Shortly after the Civil War, a young couple from Fort Smith, Arkansas, moved into a two-story log home that stood on the same site as the Walker home. Legend tells us that on their wedding night, before removing her lace wedding dress, the young bride leaned over the fireplace to stir the fire. A spark accidentally popped on her dress, setting it ablaze. Screaming hysterically as she ran from the house in flames, she fled into the wooded hollow behind the house. As she ran her flaming dress set the dry brush on fire; soon the hollow was engulfed in flames.

Her charred body was originally buried near the home, but according to Mrs. George Knerr, who owned the Walker home from 1910 to 1960, it was later disinterred and removed to Fort Smith for final burial.

Shortly after this tragic event the story was circulated

17

throughout Fayetteville's black community that one could still hear a girl's screams coming from the hollow at night. Tales of these eerie cries have since been told by hundreds of people who have lived in, or around, this section of Fayetteville.

The haunted hollow story soon led to rumors of the Walker home's also being haunted, and through the years these superstitions have been kept alive by succeeding owners of the property. Judge David Walker lived in his daughter's home during his last years. Shortly after the judge's death several household employees told of seeing his ghost descending the stairs. This new event rekindled old superstitions and once again warnings spread not to work around the Walker place.

A grandson of Judge Walker told of the well near the old home also being haunted. He recalled his father telling him as a child never to look down the well. His father explained that a "tantrabobus" lived in the well and that if anyone looked down he would be charmed by the evil monster, fall into the well, and be devoured by it. ("Haints," "tantrabobus," and other Ozark terms were created by early settlers to refer to ghosts and other unexplainable supernatural beings and events.) He remembered that his father always looked upward when drawing water from the well.

The old Walker home still stands as one of Fayetteville's best examples of post–Civil War Georgian architecture. Perhaps partly as a result of superstition, the wooded hollow behind the old home is one of the only undeveloped portions of land in the heart of the city. Ghost Hollow remains just as it was when the young bride died there over a century ago.

Lady of the Valley

Aurora, a tiny hamlet consisting only of a general store, post office, school, and gas station, is located between Huntsville and St. Paul, Arkansas, on Highway 23, which winds along the edge of the beautiful War Eagle River. The old town of Aurora, once a thriving community in the midst of a flourishing lumber industry, lay at the head of one of the Ozarks' most beautiful valleys.

The story of Aurora's Lady of the Valley began more than fifty years ago with Jess and Oney Mcelhaney. Jess Mcelhaney and his daughter, Mrs. Alvis Lewis, who still live on farms bordering the Aurora Valley, relate the story as follows:

A few years before he was married Jess Mcelhaney was returning home from an evening spent in the old town of Aurora. It was a warm, full-mooned, summer night as he walked south along the old road that ran along the west slope of the valley. Startled by an opossum that scurried across the road in front of him, he picked up a large stick and chased the animal into the vast meadows that line the valley floor. Suddenly Jess noticed a bright light appear a few yards away; he stopped and gazed at it with an almost hypnotic stare.

Within the bright halo of light he saw the figure of a young woman. She was dressed in a white dress and wore dark stockings. Her hair hung to her waist, and she was the most beautiful lady he had ever seen—or ever would see. The lady was not carrying a lantern, yet she appeared to be completely encircled by light. Jess also recalls how he thought it most odd that his figure cast a shadow beneath the full moon but hers did not.

At first he was frightened by the vision, but soon he found that the woman's beauty and gentle appearance made him forget his fear, and he stood and gazed at her for quite some time.

When Jess reached home he told no one about what he had seen as he himself could hardly believe it. A few hours later Oney Mcelhaney arrived home and immediately went to his brother and asked, "Jess, did you see anything in the valley on the way home?" Jess then revealed his experience to Oney and to his surprise learned that Oney had also seen the beautiful lady in the halo of light.

The brothers looked for the beautiful Lady of the Valley on many a moonlit night thereafter, but neither ever saw her again. Still, their story gradually became known throughout the region, and during the past fifty years many other citizens of the area say they have had a glimpse of the beautiful lady in the valley. Most believe she rises at rare intervals from the old Aurora graveyard at the head of the valley and walks from there through the meadows. It is said that she only rises on warm nights when the moon is in its fullest stage.

As is the case with similar stories of the supernatural in many other Ozark communities, the residents of the Aurora region believe their Lady of the Valley exists and resent all those who express disbelief or skepticism.

The Monster of Peter Bottom Cave

The story of the Monster of Peter Bottom Cave has been selected for inclusion in this collection for three reasons. First, it is unique, different from all other legends common in the Ozarks. Second, it is a relatively new story. Third, it provides insight into the way legends and lore originate. Although the story cannot be proven it appears to be based on actual events.

It all began when a doctor wanted for murder found refuge from the law in the forest surrounding Peter Bottom, a fertile meadow that lies along a bend in the War Eagle River near the War Eagle community in Northwest Arkansas. He spent twenty years hiding in the area before his identity was discovered and he was arrested by law officials.

When found, the man was judged insane and sent to the state mental institution. Shortly before he died in the early 1960s he called in reporters and told them that since he was near death he wanted to tell the story of a monster that lived in the cave near Peter Bottom and to issue a warning to stay away from the area. The story appeared on the back pages of the local newspapers, but since the man had a history of mental disorder it was generally treated as a figment of his imagination.

The story did stir some interest and concern among the residents of the War Eagle area, but since no one else had ever seen the monster it was soon forgotten—at least until 1966.

One warm Sunday afternoon in the spring of that year, two men in their late twenties (whose names have been withheld by request) were riding their horses down the steep road that leads into Peter Bottom. Suddenly they were almost run off the road by a tractor coming at full speed out of the bottom. The man on the tractor stopped and warned the boys to stay out, as there was something horrible living there. He had been in the field

beginning his spring plowing, he said, when he had spotted the monster.

The boys thanked the man for the warning, but decided they would never believe his story unless they saw the monster for themselves. As they rode further into the bottom, their horses became restless and soon refused to go further. The boys tied the horses to trees, then walked into the beautiful valley meadow. Suddenly they spotted what appeared to be a large white clump of fur lying in the grass near a cedar tree. At first they thought it must be a dead cow or horse, but as they came within ten yards of it, the clump of white fur stood upright.

The boys later admitted that their fear may have led them to exaggerate, but they described the animal, as they recalled it, as follows: It stood upright like a man and its body was completely covered with snow-white hair about three inches long. They estimated that its height was between eight and nine feet. The creature's body and facial characteristics seemed more human even than those of an ape. Its face and the palms of its hands were pinkish in color and were the only areas not covered by white hair. They also noticed that a strong, offensive odor, which they described as resembling old coffee grounds, seemed to emanate from the creature.

As the men stood paralyzed, unable to believe what they were seeing, the creature began slowly walking toward them and making a strange sound like the "beep, beep" of a radio. They turned and ran as it moved toward them. Reaching their horses, they spent no time in putting distance between themselves and Peter Bottom. The parents of one of these men later said their son was almost in a state of shock by the time he reached his home near the Nob Hill community. He spent several days in the hospital with a nervous disorder.

The young men's tale soon spread throughout the region and over the next several months several hunting parties were formed to search Peter Bottom and the cave. But the strange creature has never been seen again. Over the years, however, cattle have been found in the area, torn apart in a strange way. One man's corpse was discovered near his barn several years ago, his limbs ripped from his body. And chicken houses have been looted and torn to bits by some creature of unusual strength.

This story is similar to many tales of Bigfoot or Sasquatch monsters that have been reported in the swamps of southern Arkansas, the forests of nothern California, and in other remote regions. Most of these monsters, however, are said to have dark brown hair. The albino monster of Peter Bottom is therefore unique.

No one can be sure whether or not the two young men really saw the creature. But Peter Bottom is no longer farmed and only those of great fortitude venture into this beautiful valley, home of the Ozarks' only monster.

The Phantom Caboose

The railroads—working giants of the Ozarks from the late nineteenth century through the 1940s—probably contributed more to the economic development of the region than any other factor in our history. Most of our present cities, colleges, industries, and tourist attractions owe their existence to nearby rail routes. The heated politics that evolved around the early Ozark railroad surveys proved justified; many early cities bypassed by the railroad no longer exist. As with other important aspects of Ozark development, folktales relating to railroad activity were soon created. "The Phantom Caboose" is one example of these railroad tales.

During the 1930s there were reports of a caboose running down the tracks alone with no engine. These reports came from several different regions of the Ozarks. Since the stories of these sightings along remote portions of track late at night seemed to have originated in hobo camps, little faith was placed in them. (Hobos had a reputation of overindulging in strong drink.) But as the sightings spread throughout the Arkansas-Missouri Ozarks and were reported by respectable citizens, newsmen in the region developed the term "Phantom Caboose" for the strange phenomenon. The story persisted for many years and no explanation was ever provided for the caboose, moving quietly down the track with no apparent source of power.

I can still vividly recall the excitement I felt as a child in Springdale, Arkansas, when my parents took me to watch the nine o'clock passenger train pull in on Saturday night. The Frisco Depot was always filled with others who shared our fascination with the large steam engine as it screeched to a stop in a cloud of steam, its bell clanging loudly. The diesel engines of today with their load of freight cars simply cannot equal the excitement of the old steamers and their passenger cars.

As the automobile, highways, and air service developed, railroad passenger service rapidly disappeared from the Ozarks. The distant sounds of the whistle as a train winds its way through the Ozark night are now quite rare, the great era of the railroad all but gone. Today's Ozark children must travel great distances to see the few passenger trains still operated by Amtrak, and even these appear to be doomed in today's society. We can only hope that the history of railroading and its importance in the economic development of the Ozarks have been adequately recorded, and that the many folktales inspired by the railroad will also be preserved.

The Fairview Ghost

We often assume that any folktale is an old story. This is not necessarily true, as the following tale illustrates.

Fairview Cemetery is located on State Highway 45 near the east side of Fayetteville, Arkansas. A few years ago several drivers reported seeing a ghost running through the cemetery as they drove by late at night. These reports continued for almost a year and most of Fayetteville's citizens were aware of them.

One night a teen-age boy was driving his girl friend home when his car had a blowout as he passed the cemetery. Both young people were aware of the ghost stories and were, as might be expected, uneasy about having to stop at that place. The girl stayed in the car while the young man hurriedly began changing the tire. Just as he was finishing the girl screamed that she saw the ghost.

The boy gathered up his tools quickly and looked toward the cemetery. He noticed a white figure slowly walking toward the car from one of the monuments. Throwing the tools into the trunk, the boy jumped behind the steering wheel and tried to race away. But a moment before the car started, both teen-agers heard the back door of the car open. Someone or something got in and closed the door.

Needless to say the couple's fear had by this time turned into panic, and neither was able to look behind them. The boy floored the accelerator and raced toward Fayetteville at top speed. He pulled in to a well-lighted service station, where he and the girl jumped out of the car, leaving both doors open and the motor running. They ran to the station attendant and exclaimed, "There's a ghost in our backseat!"

At first the attendant thought the couple were trying to play some sort of trick on him, or perhaps that they were attempting a robbery. But soon, realizing that their fear was genuine, he took a revolver from his desk drawer and slowly approached the car. Jerking the door open with pistol in hand, he was shocked to find an old, white-haired woman wrapped in a bed sheet lying on the seat, shivering from the cold night air.

The city police were called in and the old lady was taken to a hospital to spend the night. The next day her identity was learned and the explanation of the Fairview Ghost was revealed.

It seems that the lady was living in her daughter's home near the cemetery. The lady, who was somewhat deranged, began leaving the house at night, after her daughter and son-in-law had retired. She then went into the cemetery and sat by her husband's grave. The daughter, afraid her aged mother would become ill from exposure to the night air, began locking the old woman in her room at night. She also removed all of her mother's clothing.

This arrangement worked for several weeks, but soon the old lady learned that she could get out through a window. Wrapping herself in sheets from her bed, she once more began her nighttime excursions to her husband's grave. Thus the Fairview Ghost was born, and a new Ozark tale created.

Indian Legends

The Legend of Virgin's Bluff

The sheer and rugged bluff known as Virgin's Bluff, located on the banks of beautiful Table Rock Lake in southern Missouri, received its name from a legend that has been told in the area for generations.

In the early years of the nineteenth century, long before the arrival of white settlers, Spanish soldiers spent many months in the region. During these months of Spanish exploration a handsome young soldier met Moon Song, the beautiful daughter of an Indian tribal chief. The maiden and Spanish soldier fell in love and Moon Song agreed to marry her lover and return to Mexico with him. She was, however, the chief's only daughter, and her father refused to give his permission for a wedding outside the tribe. He had selected a strong young brave to be his daughter's husband; he wanted a grandson to carry on the tribe's leadership in years to come.

Learning that the Spanish soldier was planning to take Moon Song away and fearing she would go without her father's permission, the chief sent a band of warriors to kill the soldier. Barely escaping death, aware of the hopelessness of his dream of marrying Moon Song, the Spaniard left the region, never to return.

For several months Moon Song refused to marry the brave her father had chosen to be her husband. She was certain that someday, somehow, the soldier would return for her. But after more months of waiting she realized that her lover was never coming back. Early one morning she went to the edge of the bluff and, as the sun first broke the horizon, plunged 325 feet to her death into the James River below. The chief had the tribal medicine man put an evil spell on the bluff and declared that henceforth the region was forbidden to any member of the tribe. The bluff and lands surrounding it were to be preserved forever for Moon Song's ghost.

Early white settlers heard of the legend but few believed the

27

story until strange things began happening to those who went near the bluff.

The waters of the James River below the bluff soon became known as Virgin's Shoals and Virgin's Swirl, and they were the most dangerous and dreaded waters on either the James or White rivers. Over the years many boats capsized and many people drowned in the unpredictable waters below the bluff that seemed to become turbulent only when a boat came near. It has also been reported that over the years—not only once, but on several occasions—hunters have been found accidentally shot in this area.

In 1912 William H. Standish, a wealthy engineer and lawyer, bought several acres in Virgin Bluff country. The bluff offered the perfect site for construction of a tunnel-type dam and reservoir for which Standish owned a patent. He soon had enough capital investment in the project to begin, and the White River Construction Company was formed. The Amberson Hydraulic Company, eastern specialists in dam and power-generating plant construction, joined in the efforts and building began. But over the next several months the project was plagued with one catastrophe after another. Rock slides, equipment failures, and accidents of all kinds resulted in many deaths and serious injuries to the workers. The strange accidents became so frequent that the crews began believing the legend of the virgin's curse that was told about the bluff. Eventually they refused to work.

The clouds of World War I were also gathering, and in July 1913 the eastern investors pulled out of the project. Standish folded his company and the plan was never revived.

There even seems to be a problem photographing Virgin's Bluff. Many people say that no one has ever been successful at getting a good picture of the bluff, and there have been cases of the camera jamming when someone was trying to photograph it.

It was generally felt that the horrible curse put on the bluff by Moon Song's father would be erased by the new waters of Table Rock Lake when the lake was filled in the late 1950s. Since then, however, the many tales of freak accidents, of lake homes burning mysteriously, and of other strange events in the area surrounding the bluff have kept the old legend very much alive.

Night fishermen on Table Rock Lake, boaters, and dwellers in the many homes near the bluff have reported hearing sounds resembling those of a woman crying. Nonbelievers in the old legend claim that the sounds result from the natural phenomenon of the wind blowing in and out of the crevices of the jagged bluff. But old-timers maintain that these are the sounds of Moon Song, still crying her heart out for her Spanish soldier.

The Legend of Ginger Blue

The legend of Ginger Blue is typical of the many romantic Indian tales found in Ozark lore. The story is also a good example of how legends were nearly always created about an unexplainable natural wonder.

Ginger Blue resort in Southwest Missouri was first founded in 1915 along the banks of Indian River. The resort took its name from the Indian chieftain Ginger Blue who was buried on the property, and from a romantic legend about the chief's daughter. The Indian's grave can still be found near the resort's main lodge; the marker indicates that Ginger Blue lived from 1744 to 1847.

It seems it was the custom of Ginger Blue's tribe for the father to choose a husband for his daughter. It was unthinkable to dishonor one's father by not accepting his choice. But Ginger Blue's daughter did not love the brave her father had chosen and dreaded the day they were to be married.

One day as the maiden was walking along the banks of Indian River a handsome young brave from a neighboring tribe paddled downriver in his canoe. Noticing the beautiful maiden, he turned his craft into the bank and came ashore to meet her. It was love at first sight for both of them. During the weeks that followed they met secretly along the river each day.

The brave had also been promised by his family to a member of his own tribe. He and Ginger Blue's daughter spent many hours discussing their plight and planned to run away together if they were forced to honor their families' plans. One day as they strolled near Mystery Cave a large bear emerged from the cave and attacked them. The brave wrestled the bear along the river's edge and finally wounded the animal with his knife. The bear ran back into the cave, and, determined to see the bear dead, the brave followed. The maiden waited outside the cave for hours, but neither the brave nor the bear came out. She then went to her father with the story. Impressed by the bravery the young man had shown in giving up his life to save that of his beloved, Ginger Blue dissolved the marriage plans he had made for her. His daughter was then free to spend the rest of her life in mourning for her lover.

Each day she would go to the cave and sit on a rock near a chasm. As she recalled the happy days with the only man she had ever loved, she wept. During this lifetime of weeping, her tears falling on the rock created an image of her lover in the stone. Today's visitors to Mystery Cave can still see the picture of the brave Indian, preserved forever in stone.

The Legend of War Eagle

The War Eagle settlement and the beautiful War Eagle River that winds through the Ozarks were named in honor of a Cherokee brave who died a tragic death while searching for his promised wife in the Ozarks. The story is one of the most enchanting and heartbreaking among the many historical legends of the region. No factual basis for it has ever been established, but it has been told continually since the first white man settled the region.

War Eagle was the son of a Cherokee chief. He lived with his family along the banks of the LaGrand River in Indian Territory. Se-quah-dee, a beautiful young Indian maiden, had been promised as War Eagle's wife. A large wedding was planned, and scheduled to take place as soon as the corn was green. War Eagle and Se-quah-dee had been lovers since childhood and they spent many hours strolling along the banks of the LaGrand.

Shortly before the wedding date, a trapper had befriended

Se-quah-dee's family. One night the trapper lured the girl to his fireside and told her of his love for her and his desire to take her as his wife. As she turned to run, the trapper caught and bound her. She apparently fought her abductor with all the strength she possessed, but it was not enough to cope with the big woodsman. He tied her to his saddle and left during the night, heading into the mountains of Arkansas.

Although War Eagle realized it was against the white man's law to leave Indian Territory and that the consequences would be severe, his every thought was on retrieving Se-quah-dee. The young brave mustered a small band of his friends and for three days managed to follow the trapper's trail into Arkansas.

Coming to a small settlement, the band entered the village in hopes of finding the trapper's party. In those days it was common for white men to become excited and fearful at the sight of a "Redskin," and soon a posse from the settlement was armed and in pursuit of War Eagle's party. In War Eagle's frantic efforts to evade the posse over the next few days, he lost the trapper's trail.

After eluding the posse, War Eagle's band set up camp deep in the Boston Mountains of Northwest Arkansas. It was at this point that his companions tried to persuade their friend to give up the search. Many felt that now that the trail was lost it would be impossible ever to find the trapper or Se-quah-dee in the dense and mountainous Ozark forests. Several of the men returned to Indian Territory, leaving War Eagle with only a small group of his closest friends.

The thick Ozark woods were strange and unfamiliar to them. Weeks went by, but War Eagle remained determined never to give up until he found the one he loved.

One day, while resting near a stream, the band was ambushed by a posse of white men. During the fight three of War Eagle's men were killed. This slaughter greatly infuriated War Eagle, who felt that he was doing no harm to the white men and that they had no reason to kill his friends. As an act of vengeance, War Eagle killed and scalped the next white man he came across. When the man's body was found, fear spread rapidly throughout the Ozarks. All of the settlements in the region were

put on alert and many posses were formed to search for and kill the wild renegade Indians who were roaming the hills.

With the white men on their trail, the band had many skirmishes. During these battles all but one of the Indians were either killed or wounded; somehow War Eagle himself escaped from the battles without injury. But he soon found himself alone and without a horse. He was hunted like a wild animal in the strange Ozark wilderness, and his ability to endure was undergoing constant testing. When white men got too close, the brave bolted like a frightened deer, leaping over the dead trees and gullies frantically attempting to escape the wrath of his pursuers.

War Eagle survived by fishing the many Ozark streams and stalking small game with his knife. He ate his meat raw, as he could not afford to give away his location by building a fire. He also ate the many wild berries that flourished in the forest around him.

At night War Eagle searched for campfires and quietly stole close enough to see the campers. One night, several months after leaving his home, he finally saw Se-quah-dee preparing a meal for her abductor; the trapper was sitting on a log guzzling liquor.

In his desperate anxiety to kill the trapper and retrieve his long-lost love, War Eagle failed to notice the other men sleeping nearby. He lunged into camp and drove his razor-sharp knife into the trapper's chest. The trapper's scream awakened his sleeping friends, who grabbed their rifles and quickly shot and killed the Indian.

In her overwhelming grief over the death of her lover, Se-quah-dee pleaded successfully with the men to let her stay with War Eagle's body. She gave War Eagle an Indian ritual ceremony and mourned his death with such intent emotion that she finally died alongside the remains of her cherished warrior. The stream by which they died is believed to be the War Eagle River of Northwest Arkansas; the tragedy is thought to have taken place near the bend the river makes around War Eagle Mills farm.

Treasure Tales

The Cross Hollows Treasure

The Civil War not only caused great devastation throughout the Ozarks but was also the source for hundreds of folktales as soldiers surviving the conflict returned to their Ozark homes and began recounting their experiences. More than a hundred years later, these tales of war and treasure are still being told by residents of the region.

Civil War historians and relic collectors view the story of the Cross Hollows treasure with particular interest; the value of the treasure if it were found would be phenomenal on today's market.

In November 1861 General Ben McCulloch of the Confederate Army moved a regiment of 10,000 men into winter headquarters at Cross Hollows, Arkansas. Numerous large barrack buildings were built in two rows stretching a mile down the valley. The mission of the Cross Hollows units was to prepare for taking Missouri and to serve as a supply depot for the Confederacy's march north.

General Curtis of the Federal Army was assigned to stop the advance of Confederate troops into Missouri, and to capture and destroy the Cross Hollows supply depot. Learning of Curtis's plan and the approaching engagement, McCulloch ordered the burning of the barracks he had built and the retreat of his men. When Curtis's army arrived on February 22, 1862, they found only smoldering foundations, but no men or equipment.

Because of the need for a rapid retreat, the Confederate troops had been unable to carry all their supplies. McCulloch had therefore ordered that a large hole be dug in a ridge along the valley. Large amounts of ammunition, rifles, and equipment as well as several field cannons were dumped into the hole and buried.

A post office had been established in the Northwest Arkansas community of Cross Hollows in 1843. The community enjoyed rapid growth after the war and existed until the railroads came through five miles to the west. Today the silence of the beautiful valley is broken only by an occasional treasure hunter searching for one of the greatest of Civil War treasures.

Tales of Callahan Mountain

Sometimes referred to as "the westernmost Ozark," Callahan Mountain sits alone west of U.S. Highway 71, between the communities of Springdale and Rogers in Northwest Arkansas. Rising 1,500 feet above sea level, its summit offers a spectacular view of the beautiful Northwest Arkansas Plateau. Its almost perfectly round shape, gentle slopes, and tendency to maintain a deep blue-green color in all seasons make Callahan one of Northwest Arkansas's most beautiful mountains, while the many legends associated with it make it one of the most interesting.

A large spring at the mountain's crest and the fertile farmland at its base attracted many early settlers to the region. The John Cowan, John Reed, Tom Ford, and Callahan families were among the first to settle the mountain's slopes prior to the Civil War. Many descendants of these early pioneer families still live in the region and recall the mountain stories told by their parents and grandparents.

John Cowan, who served the Confederacy during the Civil War, is credited with passing along the Callahan Mountain treasure story. As it is related by those who recall Cowan's version, a band of Confederate troops was being chased by a regiment of Union soldiers. Having gained a considerable distance on their pursuers, the Confederates ascended Callahan Mountain, where they could rest their horses and take advantage of the ideal vantage point the mountain offered. Realizing they would eventually have to face their pursuers, the group decided to hide all their money and personal belongings on the mountain until the fighting subsided. A hole was dug, their personal belongings placed in a tin box, and a large stone rolled over it. The stone was so large it took twenty-one men to roll it. Shortly thereafter, this group of men all lost their lives in the Battle of Pea Ridge. Cowan also participated in the fighting at Pea Ridge, and it is generally assumed by those who remember his story that he had learned of the treasure from one of the men who later died on the battlefield.

Cecil Patton, descendant of another early family, still lives on his ancestor's original land on Callahan Mountain and recalls that his grandparents often told the Civil War treasure tale. He says that until about thirty years ago the story attracted many treasure hunters who came to probe the mountain. To his knowledge, the treasure has never been found.

Cecil Patton also remembers his grandparents talking of the "Callahan Boys," members of the family for whom the mountain was named prior to the Civil War. After long periods of banditry throughout the region, the Callahan brothers would use the mountain as their hideout. Their mother was the sister of John Cowan, who lived nearby. Although Mrs. Callahan did not approve of her two sons' lawlessness, she always helped conceal and protect them from the law when the boys were hiding on the mountain.

Callahan Mountain

Mr. and Mrs. Berry Robbins lived and farmed on the slopes of Callahan Mountain for thirty years before retiring to nearby Springdale. They recall that John Cowan's daughter Annie Reed often talked of seeing Jesse James on the mountain when she was very young. As Mr. and Mrs. Robbins remember the story, Annie and some of her playmates would sneak through the woods and spy on the Jesse James encampment when the gang was in the region. Their camp and horse corral were beneath the ledge on the north slope of Callahan Mountain.

Doyle Reed, a retired Springdale postal employee, remembers that his grandparents, the John Reeds, often told him another story about Jesse James and the mountain. One of their neighbors was riding his favorite horse along the old road that used to go over Callahan Mountain when Jesse James rode up and forced the man at gunpoint to trade horses with him. James took the fresh horse, left his, and paid the man much more than the horse was worth. Although the man regretted losing his favorite mount, his frightening meeting with Jesse James turned out to be a profitable one as well.

The Treasure of Mill Ford Hollow

The story of the treasure of Mill Ford Hollow is one of the Ozarks' finest examples of buried Spanish treasure tales. The cave that holds the legendary cache may be found on the east shore of Beaver Lake at its extreme upper end near the Arkansas Highway 68 bridge. It can be easily reached by boat.

Mill Ford, now covered by the upper end of the lake, was located on property owned by Walter Mayes, about five miles north of the community of Goshen in Northwest Arkansas. Mayes lives on land originally homesteaded by his grandfather, who learned of the legend from early settlers in the region and told the story to his son, who in turn passed it along to his family.

In 1825, as a result of pressures brought to bear on the government by white settlers in the region, Vice-President John C. Calhoun enforced a treaty to remove the few Osage, Choctaw, and Cherokee Indians who had remained there. The military and many of the white settlers removed the Indians to lands west of the Arkansas boundary. It is generally believed that it was during this period that the Mill Ford Hollow legend was first told to the white man.

As they were crossing the ford the Indians told of a Spanish party that had come through the area with many wagonloads of silver ingots. The Indians of the region had attacked the party and stolen the treasure. The silver bars had then been placed in a back entrance to the cave, sealed, and camouflaged.

Today there are no visible signs of an opening on the back side of the ridge through which the cave had originally run. The story was thought to be only an interesting tale until the 1920s, when another event created renewed and more serious interest in the old legend.

Two men, whose names have been lost with time, were walking an old road along the side of the ridge near the legendary back entrance to the cave. It was after a heavy rain, and—sticking out of the ground—they found two silver bars. The men dug out the bars and took them to Fayetteville for an official assay. When the bars were assayed as being of exceptionally high-

grade ore, the news spread rapidly throughout the region. From that day to the present hundreds of treasure hunters have searched the Ozark meadow above the cave. All types of equipment, ranging from crude "witching sticks" to highly scientific mineral detectors, have been used. Some people have drilled from the top of the ridge deep into the cavern, with no success. The cave is believed to have run one-quarter mile through the ridge, but since it is necessary to crawl in order to enter, no one has been more than fifty yards inside. Over the years treasure seekers have spent many dollars and many hours of tedious labor to no avail.

The story of the treasure of Mill Ford Hollow is only one of several Spanish treasure tales in the region. As numerous as the stories themselves are the people who continue to tell them, and—halfway at least—to believe them.

Lost Louisiana Mine

The story of the Lost Louisiana Mine begins with nine Spanish galleons loaded with gold, silver, and jewels that left Mexico bound for Spain. As the ships neared the mouth of the Mississippi they were set upon by pirate ships. The Spaniards sailed many miles up the Mississippi seeking safety from their pursuers. While anchored in a remote cove they learned from the Indians they met that other Indians were mining silver in large quantities from a bluff along the Mulberry River far to the north in what is now Arkansas. (The story has been told about places throughout the Southwest, but the most common version places the mine on the Mulberry.) Loading their treasure onto rafts, the Spaniards left their ships and proceeded upstream in search of more silver. They followed the Arkansas River to the mouth of the Mulberry. Traveling along the Mulberry, they soon located the Indian mine and enslaved the Indians who were working it.

When they learned of the Louisiana Purchase of 1803 and heard that federal troops would soon be in the vicinity to remove them, the Spanish party decided to flee. Realizing they must leave hurriedly for their ships anchored along the Mississippi and that the large treasure they were carrying would slow them down, they buried the silver in the mine and sealed it. Then, afraid the Indians they had enslaved might steal the treasure before they could return for it, the Spaniards killed them all before leaving.

Rushing downstream toward their anchored galleons the party was followed by other Indians determined to kill them for their cruel treatment of their slaves. The constant battles as they traveled downstream resulted in the death of most of the Spanish party; those that escaped soon died in the malaria swamps.

According to the legend, the only clues to the Lost Louisiana Mine's exact location along the Mulberry were the markings left by the Spaniards. Treetops were cut away around the mine and a map showing its location was carved into a large flat rock along the bluff. But these clues have never been found, and today, as one travels the Mulberry by canoe, viewing its beautiful banks, it is intriguing to think that the forty mule loads of treasure still lie nearby, awaiting discovery.

The Yokum Dollar

The lure of silver and gold first encouraged Spanish exploration of the Ozarks. One Spanish discovery of precious metal eventually resulted in the Ozarks having its own monetary system.

In 1541 a Spanish party discovered rich deposits of silver near the point where the James and White rivers join in Southwest Missouri. A fort was built atop Breadtray Mountain and for many months the Spaniards smelted their ore into silver bars in preparation for taking it back to Spain. But, suddenly threatened by a large band of Indians, the Spaniards were forced to abandon the area.

Their silver mine and the silver bars they had stored were not discovered until 1810, when a Chickasaw Indian party seeking shelter from a violent storm entered the cave. While inside the

Indians discovered the solid silver veins on the cave walls and the sealed room of silver bars. Feeling that they had been directed to the cave by their gods, the Indians remained in the region and made beautiful silver jewelry which they traded for supplies as far away as St. Charles and St. Louis.

Around the same time James Yokum, his two brothers, and their families were on their way west in covered wagons drawn by oxen. As they reached Springfield they learned of the fertile territory available for homesteading near the James and White rivers. Their journey ended on the beautiful land they found there.

The Yokums became close friends of the many Indians in the region. They often inquired about the source for all the beautiful silver jewelry the Indians wore, but the tribe would never reveal their secret.

When the U.S. Congress passed the Indian Removal Acts it was necessary for the Indians to leave the region for lands further west. The Yokums traded horses, blankets, wagons, and food to the tribe for their silver mine.

U.S. currency was in short supply in the Ozarks; most transactions were made by trading goods and services. The Yokum brothers acquired some blacksmithing tools and shaped molds into the size of U.S. silver dollars. They then began minting what soon became known as "the Yokum Dollar." Since the Yokum dollar had more pure silver content than the rarer U.S. dollar, the Yokum coin was in great demand as currency throughout the Ozarks and was used for barter throughout the hills for several years.

The U.S. Government was not aware of the special Ozark currency until laws required that filing fees be paid when homesteaded lands were recorded. Many homesteaders tried to pay their fees in Springfield with their Yokum dollars. This resulted in notification of the U.S. Treasury Department. Soon federal agents were searching the hills for the Yokum mine. The Yokum family was threatened with prison terms if they would not reveal its location, but they held firm and would not reveal their secret. The case was dropped after the Yokums agreed never again to mint silver coins. Agents confiscated all the

Yokum dollars they could locate and left the region.

James Yokum died soon afterward. His two brothers left for the newly discovered goldfields of California and were never heard from again. The brothers had kept their secret and had not even told their own families where the mine was located.

The Yokum mine—said to have walls of pure silver and rooms full of silver bars, Indian jewelry, and Yokum dollars—is thus lost forever. But the memory of the ingenuity of the Yokums in creating the Ozarks' own medium of exchange remains as testimony to another unique part of Ozark history.

Boston Mountain Gold

The story of the Boston Mountain treasure began when Indians attacked a Spanish party and stole gold, silver, and jewels valued at $200,000. These Indians apparently suffered great hardship and many deaths shortly after their conquest and believed that their cache of gold had brought an evil spell upon them. Hoping to rid themselves of the hex, they buried the treasure near their campground in the Boston Mountains of south Washington County, Arkansas.

A Mr. Jones had grown up in the Boston Mountain region before moving to Texas and raising a family. He often told his children the old tale from his own childhood, and his sons developed an interest in the story. In July 1925 they decided to come to Arkansas in search of the gold.

During the 1920s Edgar Cayce, an Ohio photographer, was discovered to have astounding psychic powers. His wife began recording the predictions he made during his self-imposed hypnotic sleep, and he soon became nationally known for the accuracy of his readings. His initial fame came in the field of medicine. Doctors who were having difficulty diagnosing a patient's medical problems began writing Cayce for assistance. Over the years the amazing accuracy of his sleeping diagnoses was said to have saved hundreds of lives.

Wildcat oil-drilling firms also called on Cayce to help in locating well sights. Several gusher wells in Texas and Oklahoma were found through the directions Mrs. Cayce recorded as her husband slept.

Hearing of his phenomenal psychic successes, the Joneses wrote Cayce, telling him all they knew of the Arkansas treasure and the trip they planned to find it. As reported in one of the books on Cayce's life, *The Outer Limits of Edgar Cayce's Power,* Cayce began a reading on the Arkansas treasure at 4:00 P.M. on April 27, 1925. The reading outlined in minute detail the terrain, landmarks, and distances, and gave exact directions to the treasure's location.

The Jones men spent three weeks at the treasure site, but they had difficulty following the directions and locating the landmarks Cayce's reading had given them. Finally they returned, empty-handed, to Texas. Authorities on Cayce attribute the difficulty to the fact that Cayce described the terrain as it had appeared at the time the treasure was buried. The area had been considerably eroded and changed by 1925, so that Cayce's description was impossible to follow.

Cayce's psychic powers seldom functioned if the information requested involved a false premise. Since his detailed reading on this treasure came through clearly, the original story was considered genuine by his followers. Needless to say, the description of this treasure tale in several books on Cayce's life led to national interest in the treasure itself, and many people came to the Boston Mountain area in search of the Indian gold.

One such treasure seeker arrived in the region in 1976 while on leave from military duty in Florida. Determined to locate the gold, the young man spent four weeks probing the old Jimmy York property some fourteen miles west of Winslow, Arkansas. Suddenly he disappeared. After several weeks without word his parents and the military authorities began to investigate his activities in the Ozarks. Weeks later his nude body was found in the desert west of Las Vegas, Nevada. No physical cause of death or information as to how or why he was in Nevada was ever found. The only explanation of the young man's mysterious death seems to come from the Boston Mountain hillfolks. As they put it, "The boy either found or got too close to finding the gold, and its curse caused his death."

Outlaw Stories

Belle Starr's Horse Race

Belle Starr was second only to Jesse James as an infamous Midwest personality. Hundreds of folktales about her exist throughout the four-state Ozark region of Missouri, Oklahoma, Arkansas, and Kansas. Dime-novel writers found her personality and her reputed association with known bandits to be a good source of material, and thousands of western books, most of them entirely fictitious, featured Belle Starr, the Bandit Queen. Over ninety years after she was shot in the back by an unknown assailant we still find books, movies, and television specials capitalizing on the notorious lady.

Born Myra Belle Shirley in Carthage, Missouri, in 1848, Belle moved to Texas with her family as the Civil War engulfed the Ozarks. Later years found her using Fort Smith, Arkansas, as her headquarters and still later she moved to Youngers Bend near Eufala, Oklahoma, which was to be her final home. Her daughter Pearl, by Cole Younger, was born while Belle was living in Siloam Springs, Arkansas. Each of these places boasts many Belle Starr stories and hundreds of tales of her exploits are told throughout the Ozarks.

A somewhat amusing illustration of Belle's cunning is provided by a story that has been told around Siloam Springs for many years.

John Hargrove, a pioneer businessman and one of the founders of this community on the Arkansas-Indian Territory border, raised the finest thoroughbred horses in the region. His black stallion had never been beaten in a race, and Hargrove's financial holdings increased greatly as his stallion outran all challengers year after year.

Belle Starr, also a lover of fine horses, acquired a spirited sorrel from a Kansas breeder. Returning with her new horse to her Youngers Bend home, she stopped in Siloam Springs and challenged Hargrove to a race. Belle and Hargrove agreed to bet $500 on the contest. Word of Belle Starr's challenging Har-

Belle Starr, the Bandit Queen

grove's unbeaten stallion spread throughout the region and large crowds gathered to see the race and to wager among themselves. Belle hired a young Indian boy as a jockey, and, knowing her animal could easily beat Hargrove's stallion, she instructed her jockey to hold the sorrel back and let Hargrove's horse win by at least one length.

Belle paid Hargrove the $500 and reluctantly admitted he had the better horse. The next day she approached Hargrove again and told him she would like a rematch, but that she wanted the stakes to be raised to $5,000. Convinced his stallion had won easily over Belle's challenger, Hargrove accepted the offer wholeheartedly, and the race was scheduled for two days later.

As race time approached the crowds grew even larger than before. People came from miles around to see the contest between the notorious Belle Starr and Siloam's leading citizen. This time Belle told her jockey to let the horse run with all he had. As she expected, her horse outran Hargrove's stallion by several lengths. Belle left $5,000 richer with a sorrel that was now worth a great deal as a result of its being the only horse ever to beat Hargrove's champion stallion. Hargrove was embarrassed by the trick Belle had played on him, and poorer by $4,500.

The fact that stories about Belle Starr are a significant part of Ozark folklore and are still being told lends significance to the inscription that appears on her tombstone. It reads as follows:

Shed not for her the bitter tear
Nor give the heart to vain regret;
Tis but the casket that lies here,
The gem that filled it sparkles yet.

The Ozarks' Last Horseback Outlaw

The turbulent era following the Civil War was the breeding ground for many an Ozark outlaw. Almost every Ozark community was the setting for outlaw activity. Glamorized by dime-novel writers, bands like the James Gang, the Daltons, and the Doolin Gang, all headquartered in the Ozarks, achieved national notoriety.

One by one these outlaw bands encountered the law and were destroyed. Judge Parker's Fort Smith Court hung some seventy-nine men, while hundreds of others were killed or imprisoned. One such fugitive somehow survived the horseback outlaw era and ended his career of crime in a Harrison, Arkansas, bank robbery—in 1921. Recognized in history as the last of the horseback outlaws, Henry Starr is the subject of many typical Ozark outlaw folktales that retain an important place in our folk heritage.

Starr was borne in 1873. He was a half-breed Cherokee and the son of Hop Starr, a brother to Sam Starr. (Sam was the common-law husband of Belle Starr.) As most outlaw careers were coming to an end, Starr's was just beginning. He participated in many robberies throughout the region at an early age, and was caught and imprisoned many times. He was gifted with an engaging personality that always created public sentiment toward leniency, and he was generally paroled or given a light sentence.

On June 5, 1893, the Starr Gang consisting of Starr, Frank Cheney, Bud Tyler, Kid Wilson, Link Cumplin, Hank Watt, and a man known as Happy Jack rode into Bentonville, Arkansas, and withdrew some $11,000 at gunpoint from the Peoples Bank. Although a posse pursued them for several days, they were never apprehended.

Finally captured along with Kid Wilson in Colorado Springs, Colorado, Starr was taken to Judge Parker's court in Fort Smith. There he was tried for an earlier shooting and sentenced to hang by the crusading Parker, who was determined to destroy the outlaw element in the region. Through appeal Starr's sentence was delayed beyond Parker's death and finally his sentence was reduced to fifteen years in the Ohio State Prison. Once more his exemplary behavior and likable personality led to an early parole.

Over the years Arkansas authorities continued their efforts to have Starr extradited to stand trial for the Bentonville bank robbery. Indian Territory became the state of Oklahoma in 1907, however, and the first governor of the new state refused to honor these requests. Starr was never tried for the Bentonville robbery.

A bank robbery at Amity, Colorado, resulted in his imprisonment until 1913. Then, in 1915, Starr pulled a daring double bank robbery in Stroud, Oklahoma. Captured again, he spent three years at the McAllister, Oklahoma, State Prison.

His fame as one of the last outlaws of the horseback era and his handsome appearance resulted in a brief involvement in the motion picture industry. Soon, however, he found himself once more in a critical financial position, and he turned to the only profession he had ever known.

Perhaps as a gesture of defiance toward the Arkansas authorities who had sought his arrest for thirty years, Starr pulled his final bank job at the Peoples National Bank of Harrison, Arkansas. At ten o'clock on the morning of February 18, 1921, Starr and his three accomplices, David Lockhart, Rufus Collins, and Oscar Brackett, entered the Harrison Bank. Holding four employees and several bank customers at gunpoint, they quickly filled pillow cases with cash at the tellers' windows. W. J. Meyers, a former president of the bank, happened to be inside transacting business when the robbers entered. Remembering the .38 caliber Winchester rifle he had carefully concealed in the vault some twelve years previously, Meyers moved toward the vault, anticipating the robbers' next move. Soon Starr forced cashier Cleve Coffman to open the vault. Just as it was opened Starr's attention was momentarily diverted by one of the hostages. Meyers quickly grabbed the rifle and seriously wounded the robber. Screaming that he was done for, Starr encouraged his accomplices to run. Meyers followed the remaining robbers to the street and fired several shots as their car sped out of town. One shot hit a tire. This hit and a snowstorm that came in suddenly forced the robbers to abandon the car two miles out of town. No doubt their thoughts turned to the horses they once used and their greater dependability under similar circumstances.

Starr was moved to a Harrison jail cell, where he received medical attention. He refused to name his accomplices, but eventually all were caught and given substantial prison terms. Starr died four days later, on February 22, 1921. R. D. Cline operated a furniture store and funeral parlor on the Harrison square. Starr's body was embalmed and then put on display in Cline's store window for all the citizens of Harrison to view.

The twenties and thirties were to bring to the Ozarks such noted bandits as Pretty Boy Floyd, Ma Barker, and Bonnie and Clyde. But Henry Starr's death in Harrison ended the era of the horseback outlaw.

The Legend of Floyd Edings

Recognized by the state of Arkansas for its wealth of history, the small North Arkansas community of Old Carrollton, founded in 1833, was designated as a state park several years ago. Carrollton residents are justifiably proud of living in one of the Ozarks' oldest cities.

Selected as the county seat when Carroll County, Arkansas, was formed, Carrollton became an early trade and political center along the old Forsyth-Springfield road through the Ozarks. The first courthouse was established in 1836 and lawyers, judges, and court officials traveled frequently to Carrollton from other Ozark communities to administer law to the hills.

The wagon train that met its fate in the infamous Mountain Meadows massacre in Utah in 1857 consisted mostly of families from the Carrollton region. The seventeen children who survived the slaughter were all returned to relatives in Carrollton.

Carrollton's location and importance resulted in its trans-formation into a large military training center for the South during the Civil War. The city was entirely destroyed during the war, but was rebuilt and grew to a population of about 2,000 by 1875. As Boone County was formed, political pressure caused the removal of the Carroll County seat to Berryville. This move, combined with the railroad's bypassing Carrollton, precipitated a steady decline in population. Today Carrollton has only a few hundred residents.

Like most of the older Ozark communities, Old Carrollton not only boasts an exciting past but is also the home of one of the region's unique folktales. The sad story of the young robber Floyd Edings burning to death in the Carrollton jail and of the testament he left is truly a classic among Ozark tales.

During the city's era as a political center a jail, said to be the strongest escape-proof facility in the Ozarks, was built in Old Carrollton. The 20-foot-by-twenty-foot jail had walls three logs thick with the inner and outer walls laid horizontally and the center wall vertically. The jail had only one opening, a heavily barred steel door. Although the courthouse was moved to nearby Berryville in 1875, prisoners were often held in the Carrollton jail for security reasons.

The legend of Floyd Edings tells that the young man was being held in the Carrollton jail for robbery around 1888. Apparently he was disowned by his family for his criminal act. Edings was alone in the jail when it caught fire, and, unnoticed by the jailer, was burned to death. As his charred remains were being dragged from the rubble, a poem the boy had written about his predicament was discovered. Little is known about how the poem escaped the fire. Some say it was written on the jail floor while others describe its being found written on a crumpled piece of paper clutched in his fist. It read:

My name is Floyd Edings the son of old Dock
He truly dis-owned me but I am one of his flock
Hell is my poshen go necked without one sent
And to Old Carolton a robbing I went
I went to Green Forest and haried to work
They come & han-cuffed me & tuck me to court
They summoned a jury never cost them one sent
And a little courting to old Berryville I went
They brought me my supper they locked the door fast
and left me there lonely to think of the past
I sent for my father i thought it all well
He never come a nie me and i wished him Hell
No father no mother no money to spend
They left me here lonely my self to defend
The Jail house cought fire i called for help
They never come a nie me just lay there & Slep

The pleaged old jailer went after the kea
he did not find it till the jail fire burnt me
I rapped in my blanket and threw my self down
They never come a near me till the jail burned down

Death Hoax of the James Brothers

Almost every cave in the Ozarks was a legendary hideout for the notorious Jesse and Frank James, and stories of the James Gang's buried loot and Robin Hood robbing from the rich and giving to the poor are as numerous as the Ozark hills. But one James tale differs greatly from the stories of buried loot and the hideout claims.

The simple manner in which Jesse James met his fate created widespread suspicion. It seemed most unfitting that America's greatest folk hero should have been shot in the back by his trusted friend Bob Ford, and loyal fans of the James Gang's exploits were slow to accept the story. As a result hundreds of tales were told of Jesse James being seen alive at various locations after his death in 1882. At least twenty-six men claimed to be Jesse James after his death, and legends grew about how Jesse and Frank James had played a great hoax on history.

In 1926 Ebb Vaughn and his sister Sarah Vaughn Snow of Jasper, Arkansas, came forward with an amazing story. Their father Joe Vaughn had called his family together as he was dying, they said, and told them that his real name was Frank James. He explained that he had been living under the alias of Joe Vaughn since coming to Arkansas in 1885 and added that his brother Jesse James was not killed in 1882 and was in fact still alive. Vaughn directed his family to an old manuscript he had written and requested they make the true story of the James brothers known after his death.

The Vaughn manuscript stated that after Jesse's supposed death in 1882 Frank James gave himself up to Governor Crittenden of Missouri and revealed his plans. Sam Collins, a neighbor to the James farm, had secretly been courting Frank's wife Annie Ralston during Frank's many years on the outlaw trail. Frank had made a deal with Collins whereby Collins would "become" Frank James and would receive $25,000 from Frank as well as title to the James farm and to Annie. After being pardoned for all past crimes the real Frank left Missouri and went to Arkansas under the alias of Joe Vaughn. There he built a cabin in a remote region along the Buffalo River, married

This rare photo of Jesse James, left, and Frank James has been confirmed as genuine by the James family. *(Courtesy of Joe Ann Byland of Carollton, IL and Sandra Reynolds Ogg of Brighton, IL)*

a neighbor's daughter, and raised nine children as Vaughns.

Ebb Vaughn, still living in 1983, holds firmly to the belief that he is the son of Frank James and that the story his father told on his deathbed was true. Ebb further remembers Jesse James visiting his father in Arkansas as late as 1920. He did not know the man was Jesse until 1948.

In that year 100-year-old J. Frank Dalton came forward in Lawton, Oklahoma, with the story that he was the real and only Jesse Woodson James, outlaw. He explained to the press that a great hoax had been played on history, and that the James Gang had had an agreement among them that no one could reveal the truth until he reached 100 years of age.

Dalton's story stated that an outlaw named Charles Bigelow had been robbing banks in the early 1880s using the alias of Jesse James to elude the law. Members of the James Gang found Bigelow and killed him. Bigelow's body was brought to Jesse's home in St. Joseph, Missouri, and laid out on the floor. Bob Ford, who had been promised the large reward, then fired his pistol into the wall and ran out to tell the world that he had killed Jesse James.

Bigelow resembled Jesse in appearance and was identified by the banks he had robbed as Jesse James. Jesse's wife, mother, friends, and even Governor Crittenden were all in on the plot. Bigelow was therefore buried as Jesse and the real Jesse James left for South America and later Texas, where he lived a peaceful life as J. Frank Dalton.

At the time of Dalton's revelation Rudy Turilli was managing Merimac Caverns, an Ozark tourist attraction and known James hideout. Turilli learned of Dalton's tale and soon brought the old man back to Missouri. While at Merimac Caverns Dalton was questioned intensively and his physical characteristics were studied and compared with Jesse James records. Wounds and scars Jesse was known to have had were also found on Dalton. Several men well over 100 were found who had once known Jesse James. These men were brought to Missouri where each identified Dalton as the man he had known as leader of the James Gang.

Many people felt that Turilli was only using Dalton as a

publicity stunt to attract more tourists to Merimac Caverns. Nevertheless Dalton's story created national interest and re-opened the old controversy among James historians. Several new books were written on the subject.

Ebb Vaughn and his sister Sarah recognized newspaper photos of Dalton as the man who had frequently visited their father when they were young. Sarah met with Dalton in Los Angeles in 1950, while he was on a national tour. There Dalton confirmed that Joe Vaughn was his brother Frank James and that he was Ebb and Sarah's Uncle Jesse.

Dalton died in 1951 at the age of 102 in Granbury, Texas. His monument reads "Jesse W. James, Alias J. Frank Dalton." An 1882 monument in Kearney, Missouri, also reads "Jesse Woodson James."

A 1926 grave marker in the Wayton, Arkansas, cemetery reads "Frank James, alias Joe Vaughn," and a 1915 monument in Independence, Missouri, also reads "Franklin Alexander James."

Noted writers and respected James historians generally agree that a great deal of folklore surrounds all James history. Over the years so many writers of dime novels created romantic legends about the James boys that it is often impossible to separate fact from fiction. The stories Joe Vaughn and J. Frank Dalton told were full of holes and most James scholars consider them merely interesting additions to James folklore. Still, the Vaughn and Dalton stories continue to be told and argued about throughout the Ozarks.

The Devil's jewels

Nature Lore

Jewels of the Devil

There are hundreds of scenic wonders in the Ozarks, and the commercialization of these natural phenomena brings thousands of tourists to the region each year. There are also many wonders that, as a result of their remoteness and inaccessibility, receive no publicity and remain relatively unknown. The Devil's Teakettle is one such Ozark wonder.

The Devil's Teakettle is located in the center of a large meadow bordering Hickory Creek, about eight miles northeast of Springdale, Arkansas, near Beaver Lake. At first glance it appears to be only an uninteresting hole in the ground, but upon closer inspection it is easily recognized as something unique. Beautiful round stones, each polished to a high gloss, surround the hole and are scattered along the bed of a dry wash that runs through the meadow to the nearby creek. The stones are so highly polished and colorful that they look like jewels glimmering in the sun.

The legend from which the hole received its name tells that these beautiful stones are the jewels of the Devil, blown out of the ground and scattered in the meadow to entice the passerby into the Devil's grasp. The old story warns of a hex that will follow anyone the rest of his life if he picks up one of the Devil's jewels. It is said that early settlers would not even walk in the meadow as they were afraid of accidentally stepping on a stone.

The Devil's Teakettle is on property owned by G. S. Lambert, a retired geologist who lives on nearby Beaver Lake. He is one of only a very few people who have seen the Kettle erupt; it happens only on rare occasions following extremely heavy rainy seasons. Lambert has spent some time studying the Teakettle and explains it in this way:

When heavy rains fill the underground aquifers or streams to capacity, water is forced out of the hole. At such times a stream of water three to four feet deep and six to ten feet wide emerges, greatly resembling the geysers at Yellowstone Park. Directly

57

above the hole the water appears to be boiling as it erupts; it is from this boiling effect that the hole gets its name. A natural rock polishing is the result of the force and churning motion of water, sand, and stones as they erupt from the underground stream.

Lambert also relates another unusual fact about the Kettle. As it erupts, a unique variety of albino fish emerges from the hole. The fish are completely colorless, totally blind, and of no known species. Many have no eyes at all. Lambert explains that since such fish spend their lives in underground streams they have no need for eyes and generally lack color.

Although there is now a scientific explanation for the Devil's jewels, it is interesting to note that the meadow has never been cultivated and that no building or improvement exists on the property. It is apparent that the legend of the jewels and their hex lives on.

Plant Legends

Early Ozark settlers lived closer to nature than we do today. The pioneers depended directly on nature for survival, and the reverence with which they regarded their environment resulted in the creation of many legends and folktales about native trees and plants.

According to one such legend, the dogwood tree has religious significance: this small tree, it is said, was once the largest and strongest in the forest, and the cross on which Christ was crucified was made from its wood. After His death and resurrection, the tree began to grow small and, to commemorate Christ's everlasting life, began to bring forth beautiful blossoms each year at Eastertime. These dogwood blossoms are shaped like crosses and each petal has a small brown stain symbolic of the wounds in Christ's hands and feet nailed to the cross. The white blossoms symbolize purity and the tree itself the unending life of Christ.

The redbud which competes for glory with the dogwood in the spring woods also has religious significance. Known as the Judas tree, it too was once a much larger and stronger tree.

According to legend it was from a mighty redbud that Judas hanged himself after betraying Christ. The redbud was changed into a small tree and, like the dogwood, it brings forth beauty every spring in memory of Christ and the death that comes from betraying Him in our lives.

Another good example of plant folktales involves the bois d'arc, bowwood, osage orange, or hedge-apple, one of the Ozarks' most plentiful and unusual trees. Early Indians found the light weight, pliability, strength, and beauty of the tree's yellow wood perfect for making bows, arrows, and other weapons. One version of the origin of the name "Ozark" is directly connected to the bowwood. Early explorers referred to the region as the "land of the bois d'arc," which evolved over the years into the term "Ozark."

Legend further tells us that the bois d'arc once produced the world's finest, most delicious, and nutritious fruit in great abundance, that in fact it was the tree in the garden of Eden from which Adam ate of the forbidden fruit. When Adam committed mankind's first sin, God turned its fruit into an ugly, poisonous, and useless apple and thorns began to grow from the once-beautiful tree. The bois d'arc is therefore often referred to as "the Devil's Tree" and the yellow balls that cover it in fall are known as "the Devil's apples." It was thus only fitting that the tree's wood was so suitable for making weapons—the instruments of death.

The beautiful weeping willow tree can be found throughout the Ozarks along the banks of rivers, springs, and streams. It is said that the willow was once a strong tree, with its limbs reaching skyward, but that now the limbs droop in memory of the fact that Roman soldiers used willow limbs to scourge Christ.

The willow is also said to have a spell of bad luck cast upon it. Many early settlers felt that only bad luck could come to a family that settled land with a weeping willow on it, although perhaps the hex of the willow could be overcome by an abundance of Ohio buckeye trees; a buckeye seed carried in one's pocket was believed to bring good fortune.

It is somewhat ironic that the derivative which produces

aspirin was first found in the bark of a willow tree. The tree may cast an evil spell, but at least it helps relieve our headaches.

These legends are only part of the rich heritage of our natural world. One needs only to look, listen, and feel when walking through an Ozark forest to realize that each of its trees and plants has its own story to tell.

The Legend of Mistletoe

Searching the woodlands for fresh, berry-laden twigs of the parasite mistletoe plant is an old Christmas tradition in the Ozarks. The more berries the plant had the more love power it was thought to possess. Mistletoe was hung above each doorway during the Christmas season and anyone passing beneath the plant received a kiss from whoever was watching. A berry had to be picked from the twig during the kiss to seal the love; when all the berries were gone the plant had no more power. This old tradition and the legend of how the plant received its power were brought to the Ozarks from Europe.

Balder, the Scandinavian counterpart of the mythical god Apollo, was immune to injury or harm from anything that derived from the four elements—fire, water, air, and earth. Loki, an evil spirit determined to kill Balder, created an arrow from mistletoe wood. Since mistletoe grew from a tree and not directly from any of the four elements, the arrow killed Balder. His mother Frigga, the goddess of love, wept over her son's body. Frigga's tears spilling onto the protruding mistletoe dart turned to white berries, and gradually Balder's life was restored.

Frigga was so thankful for her son's return to life that she decided that henceforth the mistletoe was to be the symbol of love and to bestow love and peace to all those who passed beneath it. As a result of this pagan legend, mistletoe was not accepted as decoration in churches for centuries. Gradually, however, its symbolism of brotherly love won out, and today it is universally accepted as a part of Christmas.

Apart from its love power, the mystic mistletoe was also used in many folk remedies.

Blood clots were said to be dissolved with a potion made from milk and mashed mistletoe leaves.

A brew made by boiling the plant leaves was used to promote fertility and to treat epilepsy.

A twig of mistletoe worn around the neck was believed to ward off disease, to provide the wearer with power to predict the future, and to protect him from being deceived.

A salve made from mixing mistletoe with wax was used to treat ulcers and sores.

Young maidens could learn what their future love life was to be like by drinking a mixture made of mistletoe berries, honey, and vinegar at bedtime. Dreaming of storms meant marrying a sailor. Dreaming of a coffin meant love dying out of one's life. Dreaming of flowers meant all would go well in the love to come.

The juice extracted from fresh wood of the mistletoe was thought to soothe earaches.

Limbs from the hazelnut tree, especially those cut from branches that bore an abundance of mistletoe, were considered the best divining rods. It was believed that they excelled in locating lost treasure and water sources.

Knives with handles made from mistletoe wood were thought to possess magical properties and were considered the best for wood carving, and keys bathed in juice from mistletoe wood or berries were used to open the most stubborn locks and doors.

Miracle Waters

Few people are aware of the fact that many Ozark cities and much of our tourism industry were actually born as a result of legends. Cities such as Eureka Springs, Sulphur Springs, Siloam Springs, and Hot Springs in Arkansas, and El Dorado Springs and Ponce de Leon in Missouri all grew up around springs that bubbled "miracle waters from the earth." Some legends of the waters' healing powers began among the Indians and were later exploited by fast-buck promoters hoping to profit from the troubles of the chronically ill.

Owners of the many springs advertised their particular waters

The Kihlberg Hotel. Sulphur Springs, Ark.

as being able to cure almost any type of injury or disease. Liver and kidney disorders, neuralgia, stomach ulcers, dyspepsia, chills, rheumatism, arthritis, influenza, paralysis, and a long list of other ailments were said to be curable by certain spring waters.

One of the most dramatic of the healing water promotions was the advertisement of certain springs in Eureka Springs, Arkansas, as being capable of curing blindness. This idea originated from an old legend about White Hair, a Sioux chieftain from the north, who brought his blind daughter to the Osage Indians' magic spring. After her eyes were bathed in the waters the young princess regained her sight.

The first to promote the Basin Springs magic waters of Eureka Springs was Dr. Alvah Jackson, who is credited with founding the city in 1856. Dr. Jackson promulgated the story that his son's congenital eye disorders had been cured when he bathed in the waters.

One of the early Ozark health spas that failed was Sulphur City, Arkansas. The remoteness of its Boston Mountain location and the distance from the railroad caused its decline. Now nearly a ghost town, the city once had several thousand miracle seekers camped around its spring or in its hotels during the summer months. The unique sulphur spring was promoted as a cure for a variety of illnesses, but especially for influenza. This disease took many lives in those days, and promoters boasted that one could drink the waters and bathe in them for a few weeks each summer and thus prevent catching the dreaded disease during the winter months. The water was even bottled for a while and distributed throughout the nation as a cure-all.

The city of Siloam Springs, Arkansas, grew up around its miracle waters: the name was derived from the miracle waters of Siloam described in the Bible.

Sulphur Springs, Arkansas, still boasts the world's largest lithia spring; this spring and the magnesium, white sulphur, and black sulphur springs nearby were each thought to cure certain disorders. As a result of the waters the city grew to be one of the nation's leading resorts in the period between 1890 and 1910, and thousands of sufferers found their way to Sulphur Springs seeking cures.

As medical science developed the thousands of miracle drugs so common in our lives today, many of the diseases that were once fatal lost their power to evoke fear. Moreover, the belief in the magic-water legends began to disappear as medical knowledge improved and consumer protection provided by the federal Food and Drug Administration did away with the promotions of miracle cures.

Nevertheless it is reasonable to assume that certain medical disorders may have been improved to some degree by minerals found in various spring waters. The situation is perhaps best summarized by an early skeptic who reported on his trip to Eureka Springs at the height of its popularity. "The people there are more carried away with enthusiasm than fact. There no doubt have been some cures, but most could best be attributed to the pure air and rough fare."

Ozark Sampler:
History, Passion, Humor

The Legend of Vivia

As dawn first broke on a bitter cold morning in January 1870, a guard patrolling the grounds surrounding Fort Gibson, Indian Territory, rushed to report to the commanding officer. He had found the frozen body of young Private Thomas lying across a grave in the cemetery near the fort.

The body was taken to the fort's infirmary. As it was being examined to determine the cause of death, a most unusual discovery was made. Private Thomas, who had enlisted only a few weeks earlier, was found during the examination to be a woman. As the commanding officer and his staff were reviewing these strange circumstances and wondering how Thomas had succeeded in passing herself off as a man, an old priest at the fort came forward with one of the most romantic and unusual stories in the annals of military history. Young Thomas had related her secret to the priest in confidence only a few days prior to her death. The priest's story was the beginning of the legend of Vivia that has been told ever since by families living in and around Fort Gibson in what is now eastern Oklahoma.

Vivia Thomas was the high-spirited daughter of a wealthy Boston family. She had been educated at the finest schools in the East and regularly attended Boston society's finest affairs. It was at one of the many Boston society balls that were held during the years following the Civil War that Vivia met and fell in love with a handsome young lieutenant.

After several months of courtship, their engagement and marriage plans were announced at a ball in their honor. Shortly before their wedding date, however, the lieutenant, who had been more intrigued by Vivia's wealth and place in society than by her beauty, suddenly disappeared. He left Vivia a note explaining that he was going west in search of adventure, which he preferred to marriage and the security of Boston society.

Brokenhearted and seeking revenge for the embarrassment caused her and her family, Vivia left home in search of the lover

who had betrayed her. When she learned that the lieutenant had been stationed at Fort Gibson, Indian Territory, her long journey began. The trip was extremely difficult, especially for a Boston girl who had known only luxury during her pampered youth, but Vivia's vengeful heart pushed her onward.

During the months of her journey she cut her hair in a manly fashion and dressed in men's attire. At first her motive for disguising herself as a man was to provide the protection a male appearance offered as she traveled through the rugged frontier into Indian Territory. But her disguise had proven so successful that she decided to use it to get close to her faithless lover by enlisting in the Army at Fort Gibson. Her trick worked, and when she reached the fort she was enlisted in the U.S. Cavalry under an assumed first name.

During the months that followed, Vivia somehow avoided detection; her former lover never recognized her. She carefully observed him, all the while deciding how she would satisfy the burning hatred within her.

The lieutenant had an Indian girl friend who lived a short distance from the fort; he visited her each evening. On several occasions Vivia followed him to the girl's home, and on each occasion her bitterness grew.

On a cold winter evening during the end of December 1869, Vivia followed the lieutenant on his trip. This time she hid behind a large rock near a point on the trail where it crossed a small stream. The moon was full and she had a good view of the trail from behind the stone. In the cold, brisk winter air, she could hear the galloping of the lieutenant's horse as he returned to the fort. Just as he crossed the stream, he caught the full charge of Vivia's rifle in the chest and fell hard from his horse to the frozen ground. The next morning his body was found by a passerby and brought to the fort.

A fruitless investigation was held and was finally dropped with the assumption that the lieutenant had been killed by Indians who resented his affection for the Indian maiden.

At first Vivia was happy and relieved; she had achieved the revenge she had sought for so many months. But after a few days had passed she became deeply grieved, remorseful, and disturbed

Wild Bill Hickok

over killing the only man she had ever loved. She began leaving her quarters after sundown and going to the lieutenant's grave, where she would weep for hours and pray for forgiveness.

Weak with pneumonia she contracted from long nights of exposure, Vivia apparently collapsed over the grave and froze to death during the night of January 7, 1870.

The romantic story of this brave young girl from Boston and the fact that she was the only female who had served, undetected, in the military deeply touched the commanding officer and other soldiers at the fort. In the center of the national cemetery near the fort a large circle known as the Circle of Honor was set aside for the burial of soldiers who had distinguished themselves as military heroes or outstanding leaders. Among the graves within the Circle of Honor one stone seems out of place. The stone simply reads, "Vivia Thomas, January 7, 1870."

Wild Bill Hickok's Ozark Gunfight

Although Ned Buntline's four hundred action novels (or "penny dreadfuls," as they were called) were pure fiction, the personalities he wrote about were often real, and they quickly became the public heroes of the Old West. James Butler "Wild Bill" Hickok was one of the frontier characters Buntline chose to immortalize in his work.

Wild Bill was born in Troy Grove, Illinois, on May 27, 1837. When he was still a teen-ager Hickok's reputation and skill with a gun earned him the marshal's job in Monticello Township, Illinois.

During the Civil War Hickok was a Union sharpshooter and scout. Much of his wartime activity was in the Ozarks. He was known to have participated in the Battle of Pea Ridge in Arkansas and in other battles in the region, and he also served the Union as a spy, posing as a Confederate throughout southern Missouri and Arkansas. It is generally believed that it was during this time that Hickok first met Dave Tutt of Yellville, Arkansas.

Like most former scouts and Confederate guerrillas, Dave Tutt had become quite proficient with a gun. In early 1865 he moved with his widowed mother and sister to Springfield, Missouri. Here they lived in peace until Wild Bill Hickok showed up in the city.

Hickok had evidently returned to Springfield to resume the love affair he had started during the war with a woman named Savannah Moore. A while later they apparently had a fight and broke up for a few weeks. During this time Dave Tutt began to seek Savannah's affections. Although many Hickok historians feel that the quarrel between Hickok and Tutt had started long before their arrival in Springfield, Tutt's affair with Hickok's former lover no doubt further divided the two men. Still more kindling was added to the fire when Hickok began courting Dave Tutt's sister. Tutt's mother strongly opposed this relationship— she had no use for Yanks, especially those who had served as spies. Tutt, who shared his mother's feelings, confronted Hickok on the street one day and asked him to stop seeing his sister.

A short time later Hickok, Tutt, and several other men were playing cards at the Lyon House (also known as the Old Southern Hotel) on the east side of South Street near the Springfield square. After Hickok won most of Tutt's money, Tutt reminded him of a thirty-five-dollar debt from a previous card game. Hickok said he only owed Tutt twenty-five dollars, and laid that sum on the table. As Tutt took the money from the table he also picked up Hickok's gold watch, explaining, "This ought to cover the extra ten, Bill."

Hickok immediately rose from his chair and commanded, "Put the watch back, Dave."

Tutt ignored Hickok, however, and hurriedly left with the watch.

During the next several days the tension between the two men grew. Springfield citizens quietly waited around the square for the showdown that was fast becoming inevitable.

On July 21, 1865, the confrontation finally came. Tutt's friends notified Hickok that Tutt would be crossing the square at 6:00 P.M. if he wanted to try to get his watch back. Hickok responded, "He can't take my watch across the square unless dead men can walk."

At exactly 6:00 P.M., as hundreds of Springfield citizens

gathered in doorways and alleys around the square, Tutt appeared on one side and Wild Bill on the other. Hickok called a warning to Tutt, advising him not to attempt to cross the square if he hoped to live. Once more ignoring Hickok, Tutt started across the square. As he did he drew his gun. Hickok responded quickly; both men fired simultaneously. Tutt fell dead, a bullet through his heart. Hickok turned quickly toward Tutt's friends, who by then had also drawn their weapons, and exclaimed, "Put your arms up, men, or there will be more than one man die here today!" The men then put their guns away and slowly the crowd dispersed.

Although Hickok's trial for murder was long and bitter, the jury found him innocent, declaring the shooting an act of self-defense. After his release Hickok was no longer interested in Savannah Moore, and Tutt's sister wanted nothing to do with the man who had killed her brother. Wild Bill soon left Springfield to become a deputy U.S. marshal in Kansas. Over the years his reputation as a lawman and gunfighter grew—aided in large part by Ned Buntline's books, featuring many fictitious Hickok exploits throughout the West.

Those who were closely involved with Hickok and Dave Tutt often commented that there was an "undercurrent of woman problems" in the Hickok-Tutt quarrel, and that "women and gambling just don't mix." Exactly what the real problem between these men was on that summer day in Springfield no one will ever know. It is certain, however, that it was more than Wild Bill Hickok's ten-dollar watch.

Heavener Runestones

Poteau Mountain, named by early French trappers, lies near the city of Heavener in eastern Oklahoma. In the late 1870s a most unusual discovery was made there: a large stone twelve feet high, ten feet wide, and sixteen inches thick was found to be inscribed with eight letters or markings of unknown origin. Since Indian markings are found on rocks and bluffs throughout the Ozarks, it was assumed that the inscription on the Heavener stone was also carved by Indians, and it was referred to for many years as Indian Rock.

Around 1923, however, Carl Kemmerer began to study the stone in a new light. He copied the markings and sent them to the Smithsonian Institute in Washington, D.C., for further study. The resulting report indicated that the characters were written in runic, an ancient Scandinavian writing system which has not been used for centuries. Thus the stone was first recognized as a truly significant archeological find.

Gloria Farley of Heavener, who first saw the stone as a child in 1928, has been actively involved in its study ever since. Over the years, she says, several other stones with similar markings have been found in the area. Unfortunately all but two have been destroyed by treasure seekers.

In 1959 a Viking historian, a geologist, and members of the Oklahoma State Historical Society studied the Heavener stone and confirmed that the markings were definitely not Indian, French, or Spanish, but rather of Viking origin. In 1965 the state of Oklahoma officially recognized the importance of the stone to our national history and designated the area as a state park. To protect it from vandalism the stone was enclosed in a metal cage. Later, to prevent further erosion by the elements, it was covered.

Smithsonian experts on the ancient runic alphabet surmised that six of the markings are in Old Norse writing, first used in 300 A.D., while the other two are typical of later Scandinavian writing first used in 800 A.D. Although these scholars felt they had succeeded in determining the origin of the inscriptions, their meaning remained a mystery.

Then in 1967 the late Alf Monge attempted to decipher the markings by using an ancient form of code writing employed by Norse clergymen in the days of the Vikings to hide dates in runic inscriptions. Monge had been born in Norway and had served as a cryptographer for the U.S. Army for many years. He concluded that the runes represented a Norse cryptopuzzle that meant November 11, 1012—St. Martin's Day.

Similar analysis of a runic script at Poteau, Oklahoma, yielded the date November 11, 1017; of a Tulsa area marking,

December 22, 1022; and of a stone in Shawnee, Oklahoma, November 24, 1024.

How could the Vikings have found their way to these remote sites so far from the sea? Did a Viking ship sail up the Mississippi River from the Gulf of Mexico, then up the Arkansas, and finally into the waters of the Poteau River of eastern Oklahoma?

Scholars have not yet settled the controversy surrounding these stones and the true meaning of their runic inscriptions. Perhaps they never will. All we can say for certain is that these unique monuments point eloquently but mysteriously back into scenes of the distant past, long before Columbus was credited with discovering America in 1492.

Kingston's First Telephone

The Northwest Arkansas community of Kingston was established on the banks of Kings River by a man named King in 1853. The Madison County town remained a quiet farming community until the railroad arrived in the 1870s and provided a ready market for the timber in the surrounding hills. With the rapid growth of the timber industry, the community also began to grow. Joel N. Bunch, a twenty-four-year-old teacher in the local school, recognized the need for a good general merchandise store in the area to serve the growing population. With his total assets of $1,000 he arranged to purchase a small store building on the northwest corner of the Kingston square, bought a small stock of merchandise, and began business in 1880.

The store has remained in the Bunch family over its century-long history and has maintained its original appearance. The fact that it is one of the Ozarks' oldest family-owned businesses combined with its 1890 general-store atmosphere has made the Kingston Bunch Store an Ozark tourist attraction.

Hugh Bunch often relates an amusing story about the region's first telephone, installed in the store in 1900. A great deal of excitement was generated among the area's citizens; a man named John Rogers was especially interested. John watched the

The Bunch Store in Kingston, Arkansas

line construction crews daily. After the line reached the Bunch store there was a delay of a few weeks before the delivery of the telephone for hookup. Rogers came by the store each day to inquire about it. One day Larkin Bunch saw him coming down the road and decided to have some fun. The store had just received a new seed sower which Rogers had not seen. Larkin hung the sower on the wall near the telephone line and told Rogers the phone had finally arrived. Rogers expressed interest in using it but did not know how and was somewhat afraid.

"It's simple," Larkin Bunch told him, "just stick your head in the sack, turn the handle, and speak loudly."

"Who'll I call?" Rogers replied.

"Call Tom Scaggs in Huntsville and ask the price of maple sugar," Larkin instructed.

Rogers then inserted his head nervously into the sack, turned the handle, and yelled loudly, "Tom Scaggs, Tom Scaggs, what's the price of maple sugar?"

When he realized he had been the victim of a practical joke Rogers refused to return to the Bunch store for several weeks.

Mule Lore

Thousands of Ozark sons and daughters were clothed, fed, and educated as a result of an Ozark mule's labor, and thousands of acres were cleared by mules for building our cities, highways, and institutions. Prior to World War II, the mule team was perhaps the Ozark farmer's most valuable possession.

A whole generation has grown up since the era of the mule. Many people don't even know what a mule is. For the benefit of those who didn't experience the mule era, here is a bit of explanation: First, a mule is a cross between a large mare horse and a jack. Most male mules are sterile and unable to reproduce. The mule is strong, shrewd, stubborn, and loyal to its owner. The mule was also more adaptable to the rocky Ozark hillside farms than the horse and had better endurance for the long hours in the field. A good mule stood sixteen hands high and weighed 700 pounds. (The quality of a mule was generally determined by

Ozark Mules, Rogers, Ark.

Ozark mules in Rogers, Arkansas

its size and the slickness of its coat, rather than by the general confirmation horses are judged by.) A good mule team usually sold for about eight hundred dollars.

Along with the importance of the mule in early Ozark life came the mule "tall tales" that are also gradually being lost with time. While the women did the shopping in town on Saturdays, the men gathered on street corners and swapped mule stories. Arguments as to whether a mule brayed "hee-haw" or "haw-hee" and whether or not a mule could bray with its tail tied down would go on for hours. Typical of a good Ozark mule story was this one, one of my grandfather's favorites.

Back in the days when mule trading was big business, two Chicago businessmen decided they would come to the Ozarks where they could buy mules cheap from the hillbillies and ship them north for high prices. They put the word out that they were in the area to buy mules, but they found the Ozark natives to be skeptical and could find no mules for sale. Realizing the Chicagoans were ripe for the taking, two hillbillies approached them.

"We don't have no mules for sale now," the hillbillies said, "but we got some mule eggs cheap, only fifty dollars apiece." The city slickers agreed to buy all the eggs they had.

The hillbillies then painted watermelons silver and brought several in a wheelbarrow to the men from Chicago, collected their money, and departed hastily. As the businessmen were pushing the wheelbarrow of mule eggs to the train they were to take back to Chicago, one of the eggs rolled off down a slope and broke open. Just at this moment a jackrabbit ran from the spot where the "egg" had fallen. One of the men took off after it, but of course he was soon left behind, breathless.

"Aw, shucks," the other man said, "darn mule would have been too fast to plow with anyway!"

SUPERSTITIONS

Like folktales, superstitions fall into several distinct categories. Good-luck omens, bad-luck omens, death signs, wishes, superstitions about love, marriage, and personal relationships, weather signs, moon signs, and beliefs about health seem to be the most common. Exactly how or why they evolved no one knows, but over the years superstitious beliefs have developed about virtually every kind of event or situation in life. Although not as important to us today as they were in the daily lives of Ozark pioneer families, superstitions continue to play a role in modern society. Our superstitious beliefs cause most of us concern when we break a mirror or when a black cat crosses our path. The lingering anxiety aroused by the number 13 has led to the designation of the thirteenth floor as the fourteenth floor in most hotels and to the elimination of Row 13 on airplanes.

Many of the beliefs presented here are traditional throughout the nation, while others are found only in the Ozarks, an area particularly rich in superstition as it is in lore.

Omens and Wishes

Bad-Luck Omens

–Bad luck will follow if you carry a hoe inside a house.

–It is bad luck to lay a hat on a bed.

–You must always leave a dwelling by the same door you entered or bad luck will result.

–It is bad luck to bring an old broom to a new house.

–A traveler should never return for something forgotten when leaving home on a trip; bad luck will result if he does.

–It is bad luck to look at the moon over your left shoulder.

–It is bad luck to pull a pig's tail.

–It is bad luck to disturb eggs in a nest.

–It is bad luck to kill a deer on Sunday.

–It is bad luck to change a horse's name.

–It is bad luck to give a chicken away.

–It is bad luck to kill a spider, especially one with long legs.

–It is bad luck to count stars.

–It is bad luck to count vehicles in a funeral procession.

–Bad luck can be expected when a black cat runs across your path unless you turn and go in another direction or break the spell by spitting.

–Spilling salt is bad luck unless a pinch is immediately thrown over your left shoulder.

–When you begin sewing a dress on Friday bad luck will follow unless you finish it on the same day.

–It is bad luck to change the direction of stirring when stirring batter.

–Sweeping out a front door sweeps the good luck out and lets bad luck in.

–Sweeping after dark brings bad luck.

–Shoes placed on a table bring bad luck.

–Opening an umbrella inside a building brings bad luck.

–Burning wood from a tree that was struck by lightning brings bad luck.

–Lighting three pipes from the same light brings bad luck.

–Weeping willow trees on your property will bring bad luck.

–Whirling a chair on one leg brings bad luck.

–Bad luck comes to those photographed with a cat.

–When dressing in the morning it is bad luck to put the left shoe on first.

–When you're walking with another person it is bad luck to let a post or tree pass between you unless you break the spell by repeating "Bread and Butter" or "Salt and Pepper."

–It is bad luck to lend salt to a neighbor unless it is exchanged for an equal amount of sugar.

–Bad luck occurs when hands are dried together on the same towel. "Wash and Dry together, weep and cry together."

–It is bad luck to put a garment on wrong side out unless you wear it that way all day.

–It is bad luck to step on a crack when walking. "Step on a crack and break your mother's back."

–It is bad luck to count birds in a flock.

–An owl hooting near your house is bad luck.

–Finding a black button brings bad luck.

–Picking up a spoon by the road is bad luck.

–Burning peach-tree or sassafras wood brings bad luck.

–A rooster crowing in the doorway of a barn is a sign of bad luck to come.

–It is bad luck to step on a grave.

–Killing a redbird or bluebird is bad luck.

–It is bad luck to wear new clothes belonging to someone else before that person wears them.

–The number 13 is bad luck.

–It is bad luck to step over a broom that has been dropped or knocked over.

–It is bad luck to sweep under a chair in which someone is sitting.

–Seven years of bad luck can be expected from breaking a mirror.

Good-Luck Omens

–Eating black-eyed peas and hog jowl on New Year's Day assures good luck all year.

–Finding a pin and picking it up brings good luck; letting it lie brings bad luck.

–Using a few old pieces of wood in a new home brings good luck to the structure.

–Dropping a glass without breaking it brings good luck.

–A horseshoe hung over an entrance to a house brings luck to those dwelling there.

–A strange dog following you means good luck.

–When you say "Never," referring to something bad, you must knock on wood three times or the same bad thing will happen to you.

–Spitting on bait brings good luck to the fisherman.

–Finding a four-leaf clover brings good luck.

–Finding initials in a spider web near the door of a new home means good luck for the tenants.

–Seeing a white cat on the road when traveling brings good luck.

–Extra good luck comes to the traveler who sees a red-haired girl riding a horse.

–Each person entering your home on New Year's Day must bring something in for luck throughout the year.

–Shortly before midnight on New Year's Eve all windows should be opened to let the bad luck out and good luck in.

–A dream about death is a sign of good luck to come.

–A strange man entering your home on New Year's Day brings bad luck; a strange woman brings good luck.

–Carrying a rabbit's foot or a buckeye brings good luck.

–It is good luck to put a tooth that has fallen out naturally under a pillow.

–Sleeping with your head toward the north brings good luck the next day.

–It is good luck to bury a tooth that has been pulled.

–If you see a falling star it is good luck to count to three before it fades.

–Wearing red garters on New Year's Day brings good luck throughout the year.

–When you are experiencing bad luck, you can bring good luck by walking around a chair three times.

–Putting a dime under your plate during a New Year's Day meal brings luck and prosperity throughout the coming year.

–Leaving a cricket undisturbed when you find it chirping in your home brings luck, prosperity, and money.

Death Omens

–A needle broken while sewing a quilt means death will come before the quilt is finished.

–Stepping over a member of the family results in a death.

–A picture falling from the wall is a sign of a death coming.

–A sneeze before breakfast means a death will come to a close acquaintance within a week.

–A rooster crowing before 4 A.M. is a sign of death.

–When a clock strikes thirteen times a death will come.

–A lamp going out because it has accidentally run out of oil is a sign of death.

–A dog howling at night is a sign of death in the neighborhood.

–A cow mooing after midnight is a sign of death.

–When a critically ill person picks at the bedcovers, death is imminent.

–A dress begun on Friday must be finished the same day; otherwise death will come to the person it is being made for before she wears it.

–Holding a baby before a mirror before it is one year old will result in the baby's death within a year.

–A rooster crowing at your back door is a sign of death.

–Immediately after a person's death his bed pillow should be opened. If a circle of feathers is found therein it is referred to as an "angel's crown" and indicates that the person entered heaven without judgment.

–A green (good-weather) Christmas means a fat graveyard.

Wishes

–If two people start to speak at the same time they can make a wish before speaking again.

–If you see a load of hay and look away a wish will come true if you don't look back at the hay again.

"Load of hay,
Load of hay,
Make a wish and look away."

–If you see the first star at night you can make a wish come true by repeating:

"Star light,
Star of might,
First star I see tonight,
I wish I may,
I wish I might
Have this wish
I wish tonight."

–Seeing a redbird and throwing three kisses before it leaves your sight will make a wish come true.

–Seeing a white horse and stamping your palm with your fist makes a wish come true.

–If you see a star before dark, then spit over your left shoulder, the wish you make will come true.

Love and Marriage

–It is bad luck to change a wedding date once it has been set.

–Knock over a chair and you won't marry for a year.

–Months containing the letter *a* are bad-luck months in which to marry.

–Sweeping a broom under a girl's feet will mean she will never marry.

–Riding a mule will cause a woman to be an old maid.

–If a girl takes the last biscuit from a plate she will never marry.

–If you cut your fingernails on Sunday you will never marry.

–A girl can dream of her future husband if she counts nine stars for nine nights.

–Staring at a bright star, then blinking three times will cause you to dream of your true love.

–When a girl hears the first dove coo in spring, the next man who rides by will be her future husband.

–A manicure on Saturday will bring a girl's true love to her door.

–Rosemary should be used to bedeck a bride's bed for luck.

–Orris root worn around the neck brings love power.

–Valerian-root tea brings love and harmony to married couples.

–A girl's true love will appear if she sprinkles salt on a fire for seven mornings.

–A girl's true love will come if she places her shoes in a corner in the shape of a T.

–Eating pickles will cure love sickness.

–If a girl looks sideways into a mirror as she first awakens it will bring an image of her future husband.

–May 1 is the best day of the year for a girl to pick a husband.

–If a girl places a horseshoe over her door before dawn on May 1 the next person to pass through the door will look like the man she will marry.

–A man can throw a cockle burr at a girl's skirt; if it sticks, their love will be true, but if it falls away he should find another.

–A redbird or bluebird flying in a girl's path means she will be kissed soon by a true love.

–If coffee grounds form a ring in the bottom of a cup a lover's kiss is coming soon.

–A girl who finds dirt on her face and kisses her hand will bring her true love soon.

–When a girl's apron falls off, her stocking falls down, or her face feels hot, her true love is thinking about her.

–Marriage will come quickly to the girl who stumbles over a dog or cat, gets a bee in her shoe, sees a bird after dark, or has a butterfly fly near her head.

–If a girl's hands are cold it means her heart is warm and she is in love.

–The bride who makes her own wedding dress has good luck in marriage.

—A happy marriage can be expected if the couple sees a toad on the road.

—Looking into a mirror after you are dressed to be married brings bad luck to the marriage.

—If the bride sees the groom on their wedding day before the ceremony begins, bad luck will follow.

—The girl who catches the bride's bouquet will be the next to marry.

—To guarantee success in marriage the bride must carry or wear "something old, something new, something borrowed, and something blue" during the wedding ceremony.

—Old shoes thrown at a wedding couple or tied behind their vehicle bring luck to the marriage.

—A girl can dream of her future husband by placing a glass of water with a piece of wood in it by her bed as she retires on Halloween night. Her dream will be of falling into water and being saved by the man she will marry.

—If a girl sits on a table it means she will marry soon.

—Seeing a redbird means a love letter will soon be coming.

—The number of attempts made to blow out candles on a birthday cake indicates the number of years that will pass before marriage.

—The image of her future husband will be reflected in a mirror when a girl holds it over a well on May 1.

—If a girl eats an apple while looking into a mirror at midnight an image of her true love will appear over her left shoulder.

—A girl can see whether her love is true by thinking of her lover while pulling petals from a wild daisy and reciting alternately, "He loves me, he loves me not." The phrase she speaks as she pulls the last petal gives her cause for joy or sorrow.

Miscellaneous Superstitions

—If your right ear burns someone is saying nice things about you.

—If your left ear burns someone is saying bad things about you.

–White spots on a person's fingernails indicate that the person tells lies and cannot be trusted.

–A dishrag dropped accidentally means visitors will come soon.

–Taking a ring off another person's finger will result in a major quarrel with that person soon.

–When a spoon is dropped accidentally the handle will point in the direction from which visitors will soon come.

–When your nose itches, expect a visitor soon with a hole in his britches.

–When the joint of your thumb itches, expect a visit soon from an unwelcome stranger.

–When babies smile in their sleep they are talking to angels.

–Combing your hair after dark causes you to lose your memory.

–Rats will leave a house if you write a letter to them and seal it with butter.

–Toads make warts on your hands if you touch them.

–If a horse rolls all the way over on his back and then over again before rising he is very valuable.

–Hanging dill, nettle, yarrow, or ivy in the house will ward off evil spirits.

–Cut your fingernails:
    Monday for health,
    Tuesday for wealth,
    Wednesday for news,
    Thursday for shoes,
    Friday for sorrow,
    Saturday, a true love tomorrow.

–Plant watermelons and cucumbers before sunrise on May 1 and insects will not bother them.

–Friday night's dream on Saturday told, will always come true, no matter how old.

Moon Signs

Early Ozark settlers were totally dependent on nature; they literally lived off the land. Closely observing nature season after season and year after year, they determined that their endeavors could be made easier and more successful if they watched the moon closely. Science has since determined that the gravitational force of the moon does directly affect many aspects of our physical world; thus, some of the moon-sign beliefs may have a scientific basis, while others must be considered purely superstition. Since they had no television, weather reports, or university agricultural extension specialists providing them with the information we have available today, cooperating with the moon's apparent effects became of daily importance in the lives of pioneer Ozark families.

–Horns of a new moon turned upward enough to hold water mean fair weather ahead.
–A month's bad weather can be expected when the new moon comes on Saturday.
–Pigs should not be butchered when the moon is on the wane or the pork will shrink in the pot. Pigs killed when the moon is dark will have excess fat and bad-tasting meat.
–Cucumbers should always be planted when the moon is in the "sign of the twins" so that a bountiful crop will result.
–Root crops such as onions, beets, turnips, potatoes, and radishes should be planted during the dark of the moon for best results.
–Aboveground crops such as beans, peas, tomatoes, squash, and melons should be planted only during the light of the moon.
–Full moons cause moon madness and cuts bleed more freely when the moon is full, making it a bad time for operations.
–For best results moon signs should be followed according to these rules:
  Planting corn or fruit trees—Scorpio sign
  Planting beans, melons, etc.—Gemini

Planting cabbage and head crops—Aries
Castrating pigs—Aquarius
Dehorning cattle—Aquarius

—Digging potatoes when the moon is on the light side prevents spoilage.
—Flowers do best when seeds are planted when the moon is new.
—Flower bulbs should be dug when the moon is dark.
—Apples should be picked while the moon is dark so that they will last longer.
—The best lye soap is made when the moon is dark.
—Rails, shingles, fence posts, or boards should always be cut when the moon is dark. This makes the wood last longer.
—Eggs should be set by the light of the moon.
—Geese must be plucked when the moon is new for the best feathers.
—Sheep should only be sheared when the moon is dark.
—Wool clothing shrinks worse if it is washed when the moon is dark.
—The best time to wean calves is three days before the moon is full.
—Marriages that take place when the moon is full are the happiest. June weddings when the moon is full are the luckiest of all.
—Insanity is caused by sleeping too much when the moon is full.
—The ground rail on a rail fence must be laid during the dark of the moon to prevent the rail from sinking into the ground.
—Pigs should be castrated and cattle dehorned only during the dark of the moon to prevent excessive bleeding and infection.

Weather Signs

Since civilization began predictions of future weather conditions have been favorite topics of conversation. In the absence of the scientific methods and technology used today to forecast weather, close observation of nature was the only means available for making such predictions. Although weather signs are now thought of as superstitions, scientists do agree that some of these early signs had merit. Atmospheric conditions do cause drastic changes in our natural surroundings and those who noted such changes and recorded them for future reference could no doubt make certain predictions with some accuracy. Close observation of nature therefore proved in many instances to be of great benefit to the early Ozark farmer.

-When clouds hide the sunset, expect rain. "Red sky in morning, sailors take warning; red sky at night, the sailors delight."
-A month's bad weather can be expected when a new moon comes on Saturday.
-The number of days winter's first snow stays on the ground tells how many more snows will come before spring.
-Small snowflakes indicate heavy snow, large flakes a light snow.
-The number of days between the new moon and the first snow is the same as the number of snows that will come that winter.
-When woolly worms are fat and black in late fall, bad weather can be expected; if they are light brown, expect a mild winter.
-When a snake crosses your path, expect rain.
-When the breastbone of a goose killed in fall is thick and white, expect a mild winter. If it is red or spotted, a severe winter can be expected.
-Cutting hair or nails on a calm day will bring on a storm.
-If it starts raining before seven, it will quit before eleven.
-A ring around the moon with no stars in it means there will be rain within twenty-four hours.

–Rainbows in the morning mean another storm to come. Rainbows in the evening mean fair weather ahead.

–When a dead tree limb falls when there is no wind, expect rain.

–Thistledown flying on a calm and windless day means rain will come soon.

–Morning fog rising rapidly means rain can be expected.

–Whirlwinds on a dusty path mean rain soon.

–When dogs eat grass, expect rain.

–Cattle refusing to drink water in dry weather means rain is coming soon.

–If cats lick their fur or sneeze, rain will soon fall.

–When cowbells or train whistles can be heard for long distances, rain can be expected.

–When sheep turn their backs to the wind it means a heavy rainstorm will come soon.

–Hens or roosters ruffling their feathers indicates rain is on the way.

–Spring is here when the first robin appears.

–When the groundhog comes out of his hole on February 2, sees his shadow, and runs back in, six more weeks of winter can be expected. If there is no shadow on a cloudy day and he stays out, spring is already here.

–If roosters crow at night, rain will fall before dawn.

–Expect rain when:

   Horses rub on trees or posts.

   Robins sing loudly.

   Flies swarm in the house.

   Owls hoot in the daytime.

–When ducks or turkeys nest on high ground, expect a wet summer. If they nest near water, expect dry weather.

–When fish swim near the surface, expect a storm.

–If crows fly unusually high it means a windstorm is coming.

–When deer lose their spots by mid-July, expect an early fall.

–Butterflies in late autumn mean cold weather can soon be expected.

–The number of fogs in August indicate the number of snows to expect in winter.

- When it rains on Sunday, expect three more wet Sundays to come.
- When dandelions bloom in April, expect July to be hot and wet.
- If you throw a dead snake in the air and it lands on its back, expect rain soon.
- No rain on July 2 means it will be dry for six weeks.
- When the horns on a new moon tilt upward enough to hold water, expect fair weather. If they tilt downward enough to spill water, expect rain.
- Cold weather before November 15 means the winter will be mild.
- When frogs croak in early March it means they will be frozen back three times before spring.
- When it rains on Easter it will rain seven Sundays in a row.
- The number of days over a hundred degrees in July is the same as the number of days that will be below zero degrees in January.
- Expect the first killing frost to come three weeks after the katydids stop singing.
- Thunder on a day in February means it will frost on the same day in May.
- Thick coats on coons, bears, horses, and other animals mean the winter will be severe.
- Large crops of walnuts and acorns mean a severe winter can be expected.
- Smoke rising fast in curls indicates that snow will be coming soon.
- If many large, woolly caterpillars appear in late summer a severe winter lies ahead.
- Onion skin mighty thin, mild winter coming in.

Cures and Remedies

Without any modern medical knowledge, the early Ozark settlers were forced to turn to nature and to superstition for assistance with their health problems. No doubt the chemical properties of certain plants proved helpful in curing or relieving some disorders, and the superstitions at least gave invalids a positive mental outlook that further assisted in their recovery.

Certain Ozark pioneer women were more knowledgeable about folk remedies than others. These women were therefore consulted by their neighbors for advice on various health problems just as the Indian tribes consulted their medicine men. Such individuals were often thought to possess special magical powers.

Folk medicine remedies and superstitions must be considered only for their historical interest; by no means are any of them recommended. They are presented here for their folklore value only.

–You can make warts disappear by burying a greasy dishrag.
–Washing the painful area with swamp water or rainwater found in a hollow stump will cure rheumatism. Soaking warts in such water removes them.
–You can cure your rheumatism by carrying a small potato.
–Wearing a small chain around the neck will prevent whooping cough.
–Warts can be removed if you cut an onion in half and bury one half. When the buried half has rotted the warts will be gone.
–Warts will disappear when you touch a dead man's hand and then the warts.
–Bunions and leg cramps can be cured by placing shoes upside down under the bed before retiring.
–Night sweats and fever can be stopped by setting a pan of water under the bed.
–Childbirth is made easier if the woman drinks raspberry-leaf

tea and sleeps with an axe or knife under her bed throughout pregnancy.

—Cuts heal more quickly if you put medicine not only on the cut but also on the object that cut you.

—Nosebleeds can be prevented by wearing red glass beads or nutmeg around the neck.

—An old penny worn on a chain around the neck helps cure and prevent lung ailments.

—A red string tied around the abdomen cures cramps.

—Indians believed wearing a madstone would prevent infection and contagious disease.

—A black silk tie or nutmeg worn around the neck helps cure and prevent croup.

—A red onion tied on a bed helps prevent colds.

—A wool string worn around the neck helps cure colds.

—Drinking tea made from sassafras root helps thin the blood and prevent sickness.

—Tea made from wild catnip helps upset stomach and infant colic.

—Pokeberry juice mixed with liquor helps rheumatism and aching joints.

—Smoking dried leaves from the mullen plant cures asthma, chest colds, and respiratory ailments.

—Salve made by adding juice from boiled peach-tree bark to butter or lard will cure warts.

—Headache and toothache may be relieved by chewing bark from a willow tree.

—Coughs are relieved by a syrup made from wild cherries, mullen, and honey.

—Carrying cedar chips wards off evil spirits and disease.

—Carrying buckeyes helps rheumatism and aching joints.

—Boiling yarrow and peppermint and adding them to bath water soothes sore muscles.

—Applying a poultice made from boiling wild horehound leaves, elm bark, and honey relieves sore throats and coughs.

—Cuts heal more rapidly if they're held over steam from boiling sassafras root.

—Cornmeal burned in a tobacco bag and hung around the neck will cure measles.

—Ringworm can be cured if the sufferer finds a girl between twelve and sixteen. She must rub the right toe of her right foot around the ringworm for one minute and the ringworm will disappear.

—You can rid yourself of freckles by getting your hands fully wet from the morning dew, then rubbing the freckles thoroughly as you repeat:

"Dew, Dew, do do
Take my freckles
away with you.
Dew, Dew,
Thank you."

—You can make headaches disappear by sleeping with scissors under your pillow.

—Sulphur in your shoes will help prevent flu.

—Fresh manure rubbed on the scalp helps prevent baldness.

—Sprains can be cured by applying a mudpack made by adding vinegar to a dirtdobber's nest.